MW01641080

Issue no.11

EDITED BY:
Ianna A. Small

midnight & indigo
PUBLISHING

midnight & indigo

VOLUME 1, ISSUE 11
979-8-9919208-1-0

midnightandindigo.com

MANUSCRIPTS AND SUBMISSIONS
Whether you've already been published or are just starting out, we want to hear from you! We accept submissions of short stories and narrative essays written by Black women writers. View complete submission guidelines and submit your stories online at *midnightandindigo.com*. No paper submissions please.

Cover image: Iryna Shepetko/Stocksy United

Printed and bound in the United States of America.
First Printing January 2025

For the writers who braved the page. Thank you.

ISSUE 11

Short stories

Essay

IANNA A. SMALL

Editor's Note

I am excited to welcome you to our eleventh issue, a collection of works that represent an incredible range of talent among Black women writers from across the globe. Featuring new short stories and essays by emerging and established Black women storytellers from the U.S., the Caribbean, Africa, and Europe, this issue brings together voices that explore identity, family, and the transformative power of truth. Born from an extraordinary pool of submissions, the chosen works stood out for their emotional resonance and imaginative narratives.

From familial bonds tested by secrets, to the pursuit of healing and love in unexpected places, these works invite readers to explore the threads that connect us all.

In **"Love and a Sachet of Joojoo"** by Shari Lynn Poindexter, Ree Ree wakes with a vision and decides to use any and everything at hand to keep her man.

A married mother returns to her Mississippi roots in **"In the Company of Remembrance"** by Candace Bacchus Hollingsworth. A long weekend presents an opportunity to remember stories long forgotten and, most importantly, to heal.

"What Can You See?" by Damilola Omotoyinbo revolves around a family and divorce, exploring the balance between ordinary struggles and extraordinary abilities.

In **"Virgo"** by Shinelle L. Espaillat, a woman visits her estranged sister, who wants to re-enter the family after nearly two decades of silence.

"Ocean Belly" by Sabine Wilson-Patrick follows a girl living in a remote village that caters to tourists obsessed with the misconception that the residents are living in the last century. When she becomes pregnant with a child she cannot claim, the village's ideology surrounding purity culture and colorism surfaces.

Betty has been cleaning up after men her whole life in **"Betty's Benediction"** by Tonesa Jones. When a message comes from the sky, she heads to a hilltop revival for salvation.

When Taci finds out her husband is also married to another woman, she decides to divorce him, but the locals—her father, a judge, and the elders—stand in her way in **"Jaana"** by Banchiwosen Woldeyesus.

"The Limits of Math and Life" by Chinwe I. Ndubuka introduces a retired mathematician and grandfather whose journey home for a Father's Day celebration is hampered by a temperamental navigational system and a heart attack in the air. During the experience, he reflects on his life which, unlike math, has been anything but orderly.

In **"Mother's Love"** by Chalise Latimer, mother isn't always who birthed you. What does it mean when the one who did, tells you the truth?

On a work trip to Tokyo, Nathania Seales Oh met and visited with an aging Japanese man who had been her Jamaican grandmother's pen pal for over forty years. After connecting on a Greyhound bus traveling across the United States, they would never see each other again. Her essay, **Porcelain Dolls**, explores her experience, halfway around the world, acting as an emotional surrogate for them both.

These stories are as varied as they are resonant, but together they weave a rich tapestry of identity, family, love, and the unyielding search for truth. They remind us that while our individual paths may differ, the emotions that define us—love, loss, hope, and resilience—are universal.

At midnight & indigo, we hope to do more than showcase incredible stories. We want you, our readers, to feel seen, inspired, and experience the joy of discovering voices that speak to the heart of who we are in the creative worlds we create. We invite you to sit with these stories and share them.

If you'd like to read additional works, please visit us at midnightandindigo.com, check out our previous issues, and connect with us @midnightandindigo.

Thank you for supporting these writers and our vision. We are thrilled to share this collection with you and hope it inspires, challenges, and moves you in equal measure. Enjoy!

SHARI LYNN POINDEXTER

Love and a Sachet of Joojoo

On the morning of the third day that James Henry had been gone, Ree Ree, woke up smiling with Joojoo on her mind. After she had grown bored of solitary card games and flower-themed puzzles, she cleared cobwebs from their corners and wiped the baseboards too. Later, she distracted herself with food and wine, then ate the last of the cherry pie that James Henry had baked, and even licked the cobbler pan clean (it was so damn good!) But after, Ree Ree was all in her head. Without the power to stop, she swung back and forth from one thought—*Let him go on about his business*, to the next—*I can't live in this world without him*, before her body had grown tired of being tired and had simply closed its eyes and laid it all down. She slept so soundly she didn't dream of anything at all, but awoke with her mind stayed on roots and grasses from the Alabama woods and her heart filled with a peace. Ree Ree was sopping wet from the Harlem heat and grinning like a fool because she had decided she would have that man and had figured out a way to get him back to boot.

***

In the bright, early morning streets right under Ree Ree's apartment window, little boys gathered after bowlfuls of soggy cereal to start their daily games of whiffle ball, dodge-ball, or ring-o-leave-e-o because when the sun reached the top of the sky it would be much too hot to do anything but sit on the curb with a cold bottle of Coca-Cola and contemplate the roles they would play later in the impromptu acting classes Miss Ree Ree offered the boys free-of-charge every afternoon.

Junior smiled at his friend, Howie, as he wound his narrow arm round and round. This time he was going to hit a home run. The warm and heavy air oozed through the spaces in the whiffle ball and slowed it down. By the time it reached Junior, who stood waiting bent at the waist with the beige plastic bat held high above his head, the ball was curving down toward his feet. Junior dropped the bat. "Howie, you suck," he yelled at his friend as he touched base, the hood of a burgundy El Dorado.

From across the street, Rodney agreed. "Yeah, man," he said. "Let me pitch."

"Shut up, Rodney, you little shit, you couldn't even get the ball to reach home plate." Howie shouted back, his pale cheeks flushed and damp.

Ree Ree's knees were stiff from sitting Indian-style on the living room floor. She groaned as she rose and stuck her head out of the screenless window.

"Instead of Coca-Cola, I think somebody out here needs to get some lye soap in his mouth," she said.

"I'm sorry," Howie said, "but they were ganging up on me again."

"Well, that's no excuse for filthy talking, Howard. It's ugly."

"Yes, ma'am," he said.

Ree Ree turned from the window to face the heap in the middle of the front room floor. She had risen that morning and thought she had it all figured out. But now she couldn't find the Joojoo to save her life. It was nowhere to be found. Ree Ree had looked in the cupboard and the medicine cabinet too, and this was the third time this morning that she had rummaged through the contents of the box of obeah paraphernalia her mother had sent to her. *This is where it would be: that sachet of joojoo. Right in there with all that other stuff—chicken feet, candles, dried herb bundles--a simple little pouch, deep-red like blood and made of velvet.* Ree Ree remembered the sachet well, though she had only glanced at it when it had arrived years before. LuBell, her mother, had included a note in chicken scratch that read: *In case you need it, because sometimes you don't always know what hit you, love your mother.*

Ree Ree had called James Henry in from lying down in the back room to open the box and go through it with her. Though they had already been married for five years by that time, she was excited because she thought it was a care package of gifts to celebrate her marriage. Ree Ree had been wrong though, and as soon as she saw the blood red pouch, she knew that the package contained nothing she could use.

"What is all this stuff?" James Henry asked with half a smile. He had unrolled a tattered silk scarf and found a dried chicken foot. Ree Ree tried to snatch the dry scrawny bone from his hand but he held it above his head. "What is this, baby? Some of your mama's joojoo?"

"I don't know why Mama is sending up this stuff. She know good and well, I'm not into roots and this mess."

Ree Ree was ashamed, but James Henry had erased the embarrassment with his interest. Although she didn't practice roots and magic, she did know how to. He undid all the ties and wraps, and she explained the purpose of every item for all her life she had seen her mother work downhome miracles as if she was Jesus, and so Ree Ree also knew how to.

"Now that there is for setting things right," Ree Ree said about the herb-encrusted candle James Henry held up.

"If somebody or something is getting at you, write a name or a word down on a piece of paper, put it up under the candle and light it."

"Then what?" James Henry was grinning hard; he didn't believe in any of this foolishness.

"Your problems will disappear like a paycheck on a Friday night."

They laughed for hours that night as Ree Ree told stories about the women and men from back home who came to see her mother in hopes for a cure to all that was ailing them.

They came in sickness, or in love, or in grief.

When the package arrived, Ree Ree was angry at her mother for thinking so little of her husband and for assuming that Ree Ree would one day need its contents.

She and James Henry had recently returned from a visit to Alabama where she'd been excited about bringing her fine, new citified husband to the country. He was as big and beautiful as a blue black sky. Ree Ree's cousins had teased him about his patent- leather shoes; they had never seen the like and called them "Roach-killers," and James Henry had a good time with his newly made family. They thought he was hip, and on Sunday, James Henry bought homemade liquor from the old moonshine man and showed them how to dance the Twist. Ree Ree sat back and watched him the whole weekend, beaming every time she saw the gold-rimmed front tooth sparkle when he threw his head back and laughed. Yes, she had done real good this time.

LuBell, however, didn't like him from the get-go. The second he flashed that gilded smile she knew that he was bound to hurt her baby girl. Marie, whom everybody called Ree Ree since she was a little thing, was the last born of thirteen. She was the beautiful daughter, with caramel skin and eyes to match, but dumb as a donkey when it came to picking menfolk, Ree Ree wouldn't know a good man if she saw one, and LuBell doubted if up there in New York City she ever did. She could say one thing about her daughter--she didn't waste any time cutting the Negroes loose once she found out they were no-count. It just took her so long to recognize the signs, poor baby. And, oh yes, LuBell knew the likes of her son-in-law. Women, young and old, came to her door with tender, red rings around their eyes and pink curlers in their hair, needing some kind of magic, so that they might hold on to big, blue-black men like James Henry Jackson. Some of the girls needed a strong remedy: stand over a pot of steaming water, say, and cook up some sweat rice with it, or make a stew and put a drop of your monthly in it and feed it to him next time he comes home, he'll stay around. Others just needed a little something to draw their husband's attention back around. Those folk got a little velvet bag containing herbs LuBell picked in the woods behind her house then ground into a fine olive green powder. All one had to do come mealtime was add some love and a little Joojoo.

***

Ree Ree repacked the box now and was near to tears. She hadn't slept for two days straight after James Henry walked out into that damp and musty night and slammed the door behind him. Ree Ree got into bed all right but she was used to him now, shaking his foot to get to sleep, and she found she couldn't really settle into a good night's rest without the gentle tapping his foot made against the bed railing.

Ree Ree dragged the heavy package down the hallway of the small apartment and had to step over a pile of laundry sitting in front of the bathroom door. The place was a mess, which was unusual for them. The Jacksons had an arrangement—Ree Ree would clean and do laundry, and James Henry did all the cooking since Ree Ree couldn't boil rice and his mother had taught him well.

I should have just kept my mouth shut, Ree Ree thought, as she lifted the box back into the hall closet. Beverly, her neighbor from upstairs, had come down Friday night to tell Ree Ree she had seen James Henry with her own two eyes, creeping with a woman over on West 126th Street. Being such a good friend and all, Beverly had done a little investigating and got some of the details for her: Name, exact address, and phone number scrawled on a corner of a greasy M&Gs soul food menu.

"I'd go over there, myself," Beverly advised with eyes bulging from a head that looked too big atop her narrow frame. "It was James Henry, girl, these eyes don't lie."

And instead of saying Yeah, girl or Um hmm, Ree asked,

"Honest to God?" Because she didn't want to believe that this trash talk was true.

Beverly stopped her steady stream of conversation and said it too as confirmation. "Honest to God."

Ree Ree thought about it. Beverly sure couldn't miss much with those big goose eyes. And she was so nosy; it didn't surprise Ree Ree that this news came from this skinny, big-eyed busybody. When he got home from the factory Ree Ree asked James Henry about it. They had just finished a meal of baked chicken, collards and mashed potatoes that was so good it made Ree Ree want to slap somebody. With dessert, too, that James Henry made himself, though he wasn't a sweets man. He said too much sugar made his teeth hurt. From across the table, Ree Ree watched James Henry in wonderment. Maybe Beverly was wrong. As she ate dessert, Ree Ree had begun to lose her nerve. *Look at him*, she thought as she spooned the chunks of apple pie into her mouth, *Look at my sweet, beautiful man*. She could smell him, still sweet after a day's labor and mixed with sweat. Ree Ree smiled. James Henry watched his wife like he did every night as she enjoyed her dose of sweetness, most times a double helping, and he was smiling too all the while.

"James Henry," Ree Ree began, easing her finger across the saucer and sticking it into her mouth. "I mean, it's probably nothing but folks talking, but I just want to hear you say it ain't so."

"What you want to know, babygirl?" James Henry asked, his face a wide-toothed grin.

"Well, somebody told me that you've been keeping company with a Miss Fox over on 126th and St. Nicholas."

He was caught off guard. His golden smile faded like a sunset beyond the horizon. Of course, he had known who told her. "Why Bev worried about me?" James Henry said. He knew it was because he hadn't been creeping up the fire escape to visit Beverly since he met took up with his new girl. Then James Henry got angry. After being told what to do at his job all day, what time to punch the clock, when to urinate, where and for how long, she knew that nobody was going to tell him what to do after he left that place. At 3 pm, he was his own man, and he did what he wanted with whomever, when, how and wherever because he could, and nobody, not even the wife he adored could tell a man what to do after the evening bell rang.

"Don't I bring home my paycheck every week and love you every night?" he asked.

Yes, he did that, but Ree Ree couldn't believe that James Henry was anything like the men she had known before him, sweet-acting men who were loving some of everybody. No good dirty dogs they were, and she had left them alone when she caught them sniffing behind bitches. Ree Ree waited for her husband to deny this rumor so they could get on with their evening, a game of Bidwhist or perhaps a stroll in the warm night air, but denial crept in the background like a shadow. Wasn't James Henry a different kind of man? He had asked her to marry him before they had even necked real heavy. James Henry Jackson was a man like she had never known, and he treated Ree Ree like a queen. But that night as she sat waiting for relief, for a simple word to calm the waging within, of loving him or leaving, Ree Ree became hysterical. This was a side of his queen James Henry had not seen or expected. Breaking dishes and flinging dirty clothes. He left then. Figuring he would give Ree Ree a couple of days to cool off, James Henry headed toward West 126th and St. Nicholas, and on the morning of the third day that he had been gone, Ree Ree woke from a deep, dreamless night's sleep, sopping wet with her mind steady on a pouch of crimson velvet.

At noon that third day, the sun stood in the middle of the sky and beamed down fiery and majestic on the tanning necks of the boys playing whiffle ball in the street. After Andre made the last hit and brought his brother, Mikey, in to tie the score, the boys went in from the street-field to get a lesson and a bottle of cola like they had done all summer long. Junior had the key to the main door because he lived in the building on the second floor. That's how he knew Miss Ree Ree in the first place, just as the actress-activist who lived one floor down. She had started asking the boys questions when school let out to keep the minds limber during the break. Junior didn't know who Martin Luther King was or Malcolm X either. Ree Ree had them act out scenes from plays about Paul Robeson and made up lesson plans and invited them up for "social" studies and a cold bottle of Coca-Cola. As hot as it was, the boys didn't care who or what they studied as long as the drink was ice cold. The five of them, all sweaty with their t-shirts tucked and knotted up in various ways to catch a breeze on their young, underdeveloped chests, piled into the foyer and stood in front of Ree Ree's door.

"Coming. Hold on, I'm coming," she shouted toward the door. In the kitchen, Ree Ree discovered she had only three sodas. She hadn't done a thing in James Henry's absence, and that included going to the market.

"I've got some bad news, boys," she said as she opened the door. "Only got three."

"I'll share mine with Mikey," Andre said smiling; Mikey didn't drink that much anyway.

"And don't give Howie one 'cuz he said a bad word," Little Rodney chimed in.

"How about we pour it into glasses, and that way everybody will get the same?"

The boys coddled their glasses and emptied them slowly, waiting for their noonday lesson to begin. Today, she had promised to teach them about famous Black women who were no different from their own mothers, and who had done important things and one even got rich making something as simple as hair grease. All Ree Ree could think about as she watched the boys sip teeny sips, was how to bring

James Henry home. Yet at the same time, Ree Ree had neither the mind nor the inclination to hang on to a man who was seeing another woman. Ree Ree Jackson was better than that and she knew it. Why was she crying?

Ree Ree splashed her face in the kitchen sink, dried it with a dishtowel and grabbed her pocketbook which dangled off the back of a chair.

"Come on, y'all, we gonna skip our lesson today. Let's go get some ice cream," she said as she headed for the door.

At the soda shop, Ree Ree took the menu out of her pocket that Beverly had given her and looked at the address again, though she knew it by heart: Etta Mae Fox/375 W. 126th Street, Apartment 4A/PA3-5689.

It was a stone and brick building with bright orange trim. There was no intercom system or lock on the front door, so Ree Ree climbed four flights with the boys who left behind a trail of pastel cream.

You sure are homely, Ree Ree thought as the deep brown-skinned woman with hard pressed hair held open the door. Etta Mae was shorter than Ree Ree and skinnier too, and she didn't have half as much backside either, Ree Ree surmised as Etta Mae turned to let her into the cozy apartment with baby blue carpet everywhere.

"Etta Mae? You don't know me. My name is Marie—"

"I know who you are Ree Re. You looking for James Henry. Come on in, let me get you something cool to drink."

Etta Mae didn't mind that her lover's wife had dropped by because she was too good and ready to let the wife know that in these past three months James Henry had fallen in love and she had claimed him like a found puppy in the street.

Ree Ree followed Etta Mae inside and the boys took seats on the plastic covered sofa.

"Actually, I'm not looking for James Henry," Ree Ree continued, feeling a little uneasy for the whopping lie she was about to tell. "I came to drop off the kids. If you want him, you can have him, Etta Mae, but it's a package deal."

Etta Mae turned to face Ree Ree. "Say what now?"

"I'll have their things sent over or you and James Henry can come by the house when he gets in from work. Whatever suits you."

Etta Mae surveyed the five boys. They were all some variation of brown, and could have been James Henry's kids, except for Howie who was just as bright white as he wanted to be.

She pointed.

"Him, too. That James Henry's boy?"

Sitting between Andre and Little Rodney, Howie's skin paled against the deep hazelnut like mayonnaise between two pieces of toasted wheat bread.

"Yes, indeed," Ree Ree smiled. "That's Howie, he takes after my side of the family."

Etta Mae didn't question it, Ree Ree was pretty light-skinned, and Etta Mae knew how that went. She had folks in her own family so light they could have been passing.

"James Henry told me he had a wife," Etta Mae admitted, "but the kids, he didn't say nothing about all that."

"Well, they're right here for you to see." Ree Ree beamed with a mother's pride. "Listen, I'm gonna head back to the house. James Henry should be here soon, right? You all can work this out however you want to."

As Ree Ree stepped to the door, Etta Mae plopped down into a chair and watched the boys drip ice cream all over her baby blue shag.

"Y'all better behave. Listen to Miss Etta Mae, hear?"

Ree Ree laughed out loud when she reached the street. Etta Mae was a bigger fool than she thought. *I bet she'll think twice before she messes with somebody else's husband,* Ree Ree said to herself as she sashayed down 126th toward the subway.

***

It was the longest and most miserable hour of their lives. The boys tried to keep still, but after their ice cream cones had been licked and sucked and chewed up, they found themselves with nothing to do with their hands. Junior wanted to go outside. His legs were hot and sticking to the sofa cover. Andre picked up a porcelain figurine of a collie off the coffee table and tossed it in the air. Mikey offered to play with him, and by the time James Henry walked in the door the five of them were enthralled in an amusing game of 'Catch the Collie' that Etta Mae, for the life of her, could not control.

"What in the world?" James Henry stopped dead in his tracks.

Rodney was in the middle of a toss to Howie. When Howie heard James Henry's voice he ran to him screaming, "Daddy," and hugged him around the waist.

James Henry looked over at Etta Mae standing in the doorway with her hands on her hips and a garbage bag full of his things at her feet.

***

It was past five o'clock when Ree Ree heard the dead bolt click. She was sitting on the bed reading *Ebony*. James Henry walked to the backroom and stood in the doorway, looking at his wife. Ree Ree turned a page. The two were silent for so long that Ree Ree started to feel funny and had to look up.

"You know you crazy, don't you, woman?"

"Crazy 'bout you."

"Etta Mae didn't know what to do with herself," James Henry told her. "I knew she wasn't the brightest star in the night sky, but only a fool would believe that that little Jewish boy is mine, I don't care how big his afro is."

From deep in their bowels, they hollered and laughed laughs that made their eyes wet. And everything was fine. James Henry made love to Ree Ree like it was the first time he had ever known her. And with his woman in his arms, James Henry lulled off to sleep, his foot tapped against the bed railing, and Ree Ree slept like a bear cub in winter.

In the morning, she rose early and put a pot of coffee on before James Henry left for work. James Henry grabbed her around the waist when she walked him to the door and pulled her to his chest. It was good to be back home where he belonged.

Ree Ree hummed all morning, This Crazy Thing Called Love, while she prepared dinner for a change to celebrate James Henry's homecoming. She was making chili, which was the only thing that she knew how to make that wasn't too salty or too burnt or too terrible to eat.

The chili was simmering in a pot when Ree Ree went to take out the ingredients for a small pan of cornbread: sugar, eggs, milk, cornmeal, flour. Ree Ree reached into the cabinet above the stove and retrieved the baking soda and the large silver canister with *Sugar* written across it. As she pulled it off the shelf, Ree Ree's eyes caught a glimpse of crimson peeking out from beneath the raised corner of contact paper. She placed the sugar on the counter and pulled out the remaining canisters to peel back the sticky paper back a little more. And there it was, ducked down in the corner hiding like a child, the crime-scene crimson sachet of Joojoo.

"Now, I've been looking all over for you," Ree Ree said holding the almost empty pouch. "What in the world are you doing in here?"

When it hit her, Ree Ree had to sit herself down.

CANDACE BACCHUS HOLLINGSWORTH

In the Company of Remembrance

God, I need a lifeline.

She wasn't necessarily speaking *to* God, or at least, not the version she'd created in her mind since her childhood years at Holy Everlasting Baptist Church. That God was embodied—in fact, there was little separation between the image in her mind and the pictures of white Jesus that were emblazoned in the center of porcelain plates with scalloped gold edges. She was thinking aloud using words that were familiar despite how foreign they felt. In Shelby's world, she had become her own savior. Up to that point, she could rely on herself to pull through every rough patch. She could journal her fears and sorrows away, or at least until she'd tied a tight enough knot along her fragile seams to keep them from unraveling. Her friends knew she had moments where she felt unsure or too burdened by work or her children, and they were there to help her commiserate and, at times, fix the problem. Neither of these—the journal or her friends—could do what she wanted most. She was desperate to feel worthy of more than a hard time. They say we all call on God at some point.

Shelby tightened her grip around the taut leather of the steering wheel as she expertly navigated the winding road in Hernando, Mississippi. Her father had told her that this area where he grew up was called Dark Corner. Even though Dark Corner likely spanned about three square miles, this turn, with its deep apex and canopy of kudzu, signaled to her that she'd arrived.

More than five years had passed since she traveled alone, and equally as many since she paid a visit to the family home. The road leading to the house where her grandparents raised their children and hosted dozens of grandchildren for family dinners was freshly paved. There were no markings, however. It was paved for the convenience of those who inhabited Dark Corner, the ones who knew her twists and curves, not the ones who needed instructions on how to stay safe. Those interlopers were not far away, though.

Although the place felt the same, little changes emerged from unexpected places. Here and there, an additional house took up space between neighbors that would have previously been ample space for children to play, running a quarter of a mile just to see if so-and-so was home. Wooden fences to delineate mine from theirs now took the place of the barbed wire that separated cows from humans. Landowners were now homeowners who tended to curb appeal with surgical precision. These scenes, indistinguishable to an untrained eye, scrolled past the driver's side window as Shelby drove the respectable 15 miles per hour to what was her grandparents' home.

She turned onto the red dirt driveway and crept slowly up the path until it opened to the five acres of land that would be her home for the weekend. The house stood in the distance, unchanged by neither time nor intention, waiting to welcome her home.

She opened the car door, and as her body unfolded, she took a deep breath; even the air was comforting. It was unseasonably cold this November. Instead of sunshine, the sun cast shadows across the grass, covering the lawn in shades of green, brown, and grey. It was odd. Back in Philadelphia, these would be signs of abandonment. The same house over a thousand miles away would scream, "Do not enter; there is no love here." Yet, here, it was an invitation to be still and find yourself. In her case, it was a command.

The week prior, she could barely get through her monthly session with Arya, her therapist. Her thoughts would travel from their home behind her eyes down to her throat and emerge as gasps for air and tears in the corners of her eyes.

Arya stared at her through the screen, waiting patiently for Shelby to be brave enough to say what she needed to say. In their work together, Arya was helping Shelby discover who she was without others' expectations. In that, Shelby had to understand her purpose and believe there was a reason for her existence. She had to identify her unique gift, and that was the hard part.

At the start of their first session, Arya asked, "Who are you?"

"Umm...I'm Shelby. I'm forty years old. I'm married with three children. Let me see...I work at a nonprofit downtown—"

"I appreciate the LinkedIn summary, but I asked you who you are," Arya interrupted.

That had been their relationship for the four years since. They did this dance of avoidance and stern correction, and it was hard to tell whether Shelby's responses were honest or if they were her way of testing Arya's willingness to probe further. Somewhere along the journey of her life, Shelby had come to equate inquiry with interest and interest with love. She never questioned why she needed her therapist to love her, because it was no different from what she wanted from everyone she encountered.

Last Tuesday morning, she sat, voiceless, unable to answer the latest question along her path to self-discovery.

If you could have a superpower, what would it be?

She sat in deep thought, pondering the question. The word *invisible* traveled from her head down to her stomach, where it tumbled around with *teleportation* and *shapeshifting* until it erupted from her heart.

"Visible. I would be visible," she replied with quivering

lips as the tears released themselves onto her cheeks.

They sat with Shelby's truth and weaved in and out of her memories to identify when she first felt invisible and who she wished, most fervently, noticed her. With Arya's guidance, they decided that Shelby would go back to the place she considered home. Her assignment was to go home and, in solitude, allow herself to be seen. So here she was, states away, standing at the threshold with groceries in hand, ready to meet her superpower.

For the next three days, she only needed to care for herself and could spend the entirety of that time in silence if she wished. The door was unlocked, the way it had always been growing up. Despite the many offers the family, Shelby's mother, aunts, and uncles had received in the decade since her grandparents' death—some north of one million dollars—they made the conscious decision to keep the family home. This land belonged to them, all their children, and their children, too, with only one house rule: Come as you are and leave it how you found it, or better.

She grabbed a mason jar from the open shelf and filled it with cool, crisp water from the faucet before placing a single, magenta-toned pansy stem inside. She turned to put away the groceries. Granola in the cabinet. Bread and coffee on the countertop. Bananas on the windowsill. Eggs, oat milk, half and half, and coconut yogurt in the refrigerator. She amused herself at the idea that such meager provisions and the accompanying $63 tab would have offered more than a day's breakfast for her family of five. Cell phone in hand, she fired off text messages to let her children and her best friends know that she would be turning her phone off, leaving them the number to the house phone; the number had not changed since she was a little girl. She waited a few minutes before shutting down her phone entirely, just in case there was one final message. This would be the hardest part of her assignment. She lived in and with her phone.

The sun began to find its home across the field and behind the winter-barren trees, flipping her mind's switch to memories she'd stored away. This time of the day decades ago was the point when she and all her cousins would return, one-by-one, to their grandmother's kitchen table for dinner after washing up and cleansing their bodies of the day's dirt, ticks, pine needles, and chiggers. Today, she sat at the same table intentionally alone, with a dinner of toast and two fried eggs with cracked pepper. Over the years, she had trained herself to appreciate simple, savory dishes like this one to help shed nearly eighty pounds packed on to the all the "baby fat" that never disappeared as her mother promised.

Shelby thought about how she, as the youngest of the clan, would get a little touch of sugar in her rice because that was how her mother made it. There were always small differences like those: a spoonful of sugar here, a diagonal cut across her sandwich, the prettiest, deepest red wedge of watermelon, strawberries in her Corn Flakes because she hated bananas then, and a little drizzle of honey trailed across cucumber salad at dinner to take away the vinegar's bite. Tonight, these memories traveled through her body differently. Where they used to feel cold, they now felt warm. Memory is a curious thing. She always felt that she was treated differently from her other cousins. She often easily remembered the times that she felt like an outsider because she was browner, or fatter, or because her hair wasn't as long. For the first time, she remembered young Shelby as a little girl who was cared for and looked after as her unique, individual self.

Okay, I see what you did there.

The next morning, the sun peeked through the sheer curtains, gently nudging her to wake up and greet the day. Shelby lay in bed, tucked underneath sturdy yet soft sheets that somehow still smelled like a summer day even though they had probably last hung outdoors twenty years before.

Everyone had chores during the summer, even the young ones. By the time Shelby was old and tall enough to hang the clothes on the line, her summers were spent on university campuses learning and collecting entries for what would become her resume. Her arms, however, were long enough to reach the bottoms of everything hung—t-shirts, sheets, towels, and pillowcases—so she got to yank each piece down. The week's laundry relied on her completing that task. Everyone else had a partner. Two cousins hung the laundry. Two cousins did the dishes together. Each morning, two cousins made the beds and folded the blankets that made up the many pallets across the floors. Yet, Shelby completed her chore alone, wishing she had someone to do it with. She wanted to let tears well up in her eyes because she had become accustomed to being the orphan in her own stories; she often found comfort in the familiar feeling of being an outcast.

Like a wave, scenes from a past returned. She recalled the way her grandmother would say, "I can finish once Shelby finishes bringing in the laundry." Grandmother gave Shelby something that only she could be proud of and always gave her credit. Shelby spent the rest of the day thinking about how much she actually despised group projects. She'd always excelled in solo endeavors: Spelling Bee champion, winning essay and art contests, and making principal's Honor Roll. She knew *how* to be a team player, of course, but she enjoyed the thrill of being acknowledged for her work. She thought of the long summer days spent playing Hide and Seek, where she was always found last, not because she was particularly good at hiding, but because the big kids enjoyed playing the game without her. Those days often ended with her grandmother telling her, "Seeking might be a challenge, but at least then you don't have to worry about whether folks want to find you or not." And so, Shelby lived her life in charge. She did not seek credit, but that wasn't necessary when there was no one else capable of taking it from you.

This was Shelby's first time in this house without anyone else. The silence was unfamiliar, though not uncomfortable. Dressed in her quilted housecoat and slippers, a fresh mug of coffee in hand, she strolled from room to room, snapping photos in her mind's eye of the details that she had allowed herself to forget. She did not want to forget anymore, nor did she want to misremember.

She took in the view from each window. From one room, she saw pasture, and from the next, she saw overgrown trees and bushes. The living room window was the only one that provided an uninterrupted view of the handmade flower beds that were home to her grandmother's rose bushes. She knew the beauty that would come next spring: blossoms of pink and red that never quite looked the same as the roses you could find in grocery stores. Someone who did not know what was, one of those people who recently discovered Dark Corner, would make the mistake of cutting away or pulling up the small bushels of twigs. Barrenness had never made her so content.

She moved along to the family room and stood in the doorframe as her eyes darted from wall to wall.

The Comtoise clock, a gift from her aunts and uncles, stood in its place in the corner. On the opposite wall, the empty fireplace with a thin layer of gray ash covering the hearth—undoubtedly remains from the previous winter—begged her to bring it back to life. She placed her mug down on the coffee table, slid on her worn-over Uggs, and ventured outdoors to find wood.

Someone, perhaps one of her uncles, had stacked firewood just outside the door in the same way it'd been done for decades, so she only needed to find kindling. She walked around the perimeter of the property, picking up sticks here and there. Although she walked with purpose, her gait slowed as she came upon the backdrops to scenes of her youth. Each step was a new act.

The dogwood tree was "base" for the complicated games of Hide and Seek. The empty farm shed in the far corner was the meeting room where the cousins gathered to play school. The honeysuckle bushes provided mid-afternoon refreshment in the heat of the afternoon sun when it was still too early to be allowed indoors. The clothesline's poles, worn and rusted from over sixty years of use, stood between her and the shortcut to the home's side door. Her forehead was now at least a foot above its highest point, and she smiled, imagining that little girl whose arms could only reach so high.

Shelby climbed the brick steps and opened the door with a modest pile of small sticks cradled in her left arm and retreated back inside.

She took care to start the fire. She tore the orange plastic from an old newspaper and slowly unfolded the stiff pages that had dried from spending too much time in the rain, only to crumple them up again and stick the small balls of news under the iron grates. She placed the twigs she'd collected from her morning walk about the property and placed several logs, crosshatched style, on top of them. She lit the paper and stood back to admire her work. Shelby spent the rest of the day sipping coffee, peeling fruit, and cracking pecans in front of the fireplace until sunset.

On this final night, Shelby questioned whether this trip served the purpose it intended. Even still, she wanted to wrap up her time doing something that felt familiar, so she decided to make her grandmother's egg custard pie. Her grandmother did not share recipes in any formal way. You had to catch her on the days she felt like having company in the kitchen and just sit and watch. Shelby spied her way onto her grandmother's egg custard pie recipe one summer evening when she found herself alone with just her grandmother and grandfather. Her other cousins had left for an out-of-town retreat with the church, one that her family could not afford. At first, she cried at being left behind until she summoned the courage to sit across from her grandmother as she cooked. Her grandmother never told her to find something to do—her nice way of saying she preferred to be left alone—and so she sat, observed, and recorded her grandmother's handiwork in her mind.

Shelby pulled all the ingredients to the counter and went about crafting her grandmother's pie in her grandmother's kitchen. As she whisked the sugar and egg yolks together under the small countertop light, she saw her younger self sitting across from her. Every emotion she knew, she felt that night sitting across from her grandmother, she saw them on her younger face. The admiration, the love she felt, the feeling of being included, she saw it all as young Shelby smiled back at her.

You never eat egg custard pie right out of the oven. It tastes the best after it's had the chance to sit and come to room temperature. Although the ingredients are easy and typically always on hand, it's the kind of dessert you plan to serve. If your guests are able to eat it after their dinner, they know it was made with intention. And so it was for Shelby. She planned to have coffee and a slice of pie for breakfast on her last day at the family home. It was the proper way to conclude her visit, she figured. She pulled the pie out of the oven, placed it on a knitted potholder, switched on the nightlight over the stove, and prepared for bed.

The next morning, Shelby busied herself with the tasks to close the house and make it ready for whoever the next visitor would be. She cleaned the fireplace of the ashes from the day before, ran the dishwasher, washed and dried the bed linens and towels, and made the bed. There wasn't much to pack into her little bag because she spent the weekend in the same housecoat.

After she got dressed for the drive back to the Memphis airport, she set the table for her final meal. She skipped the placemat just in case she spilled a little coffee because she would not have time to wash it afterward. Instead, she laid down two paper towels and placed a small dessert plate from the cabinet on top, along with a fork and butter knife. She brought the pie and potholder from the countertop and set them both at a respectable 11 o'clock position beside her grandmother's pie server. Remembering the times she and her grandmother spent having tea while the other cousins were away, Shelby decided to use the same small porcelain teacup and saucer they would use from the China cabinet. She twisted the latch on the cabinet, careful not to disturb the contents as she opened the door.

When Shelby reached for the cup housed on the far-right side of the cabinet, she saw a small manila envelope tucked between the gold edges of the plates and the cabinet's glass walls. On the front of the envelope, she saw "Shelby" written in perfect cursive writing that she knew belonged to her grandmother. Although her fingers trembled as she pulled the envelope from its home, she steadied herself long enough to make it back to the small kitchen table. She undid the brads on the back and separated the flap from the rest of the package. Inside, she found pictures of herself, one for every year of her life. When she flipped each one over, on the back she saw her grandmother's writing indicating Shelby's age and one to five words seemingly describing a memory.

2 yrs old. Vaseline not lotion.

5 yrs old, No blackberries.

Age 14. Summer program at Duke.

17 yrs. Graduation with honors.

Age 24. First job.

Shelby held each photo, tenderly kissing each one from age 1 to 24 before returning it to the envelope, and her tears flowed. She cried because she missed her grandmother, and she cried because she could feel her grandmother was there. Mostly, she cried because she realized she had never been invisible after all. She sat silently and peacefully without worry or wonder and savored a slice of egg pie and a cup of coffee.

In honor of the house rule, she took a pen and piece of paper from the gossip bench and carefully wrote the recipe for Grandmother's Egg Custard Pie and affixed it to the refrigerator with a pear magnet.

With her bag in hand and all of the dishes empty and returned to their place, Shelby left and closed the door behind her.

God, I thank you.

DAMILOLA OMOTOYINBO

What Can You See?

I had my first kiss three years after my parents divorced. I was fourteen. We were living in our food canteen at the section of Bodija market where fabrics are sold.

My mum calls me Adeife because she believes children are the crown of love and Dad calls me by my Grandma's maiden name, Lydia. She died a month after the divorce—exactly a year after the car crash that killed my brother. I have a few memories of her and the one that cleaved to the walls of my heart was of her walking into the house with a pregnant woman and a girl my age.

Grandma introduced her as my father's new woman. She did not call her a wife.

"Mummy Adeife, erm, that woman is carrying your husband's son." Grandma ordered the woman and the girl to sit. My father's eyes darted from a confused Mum to Grandma.

"Akin, what is going on here? Tell me this is all a joke." He dipped his hands into his pocket as if to bring out something.

"Mummy Adeife, your husband is a good man, he can take care of all of you."

"Akin, this must be a joke," Mum said, as if she had not heard Grandma. As if the old woman was only a brick, a sculpture that did not deserve her attention. Dad did not speak, his lips twitched. He moved toward Mum to hold her, but stopped halfway.

Mum left the living room shouting that nothing will make her leave her husband's house and any new woman who came was only a visitor who would leave empty-handed. That was the first time Grandma did not eat during a visit, the first time Mum did not kneel to greet her. I had believed there would be another time when Grandma would eat and we would all smile like we used to. But the next time I saw her, she was in a coffin, a stiff smile plastered on her face like someone who fought the world and won.

Dad enrolled the girl who came with the pregnant woman in the same school I attended. Her name was Bimpe, she was the first child of the woman, and had a different father. Dad told me to treat her like a sister, and the baby, once he was born, like a brother.

"For peace to reign in this house, treat them like family."

I wanted to ask how he knew the gender of the unborn baby but I did not. I was eager to experience having a brother. I used to have one, he was born on a Sunday, at the church clinic.

Everything went the way it had been until the woman gave birth. While pregnant, she smiled often and avoided my mother. But whenever Mum was away from home, she would cook and give me food. The baby was named Ariyo, he had the lips, nose, and little black ears of my father. During the naming ceremony, Mum stared at the baby as if she had finally found living evidence of her failure.

Dad began the comparison. First, it sounded like a joke.

He claimed Bimpe's name was well picked, it suited her. Bimpe had enough flesh in the right places. Not in excess, not scanty, just enough—spotless caramel skin and hair curling to the back of her neck.

I was the opposite—slim and flat like a plank, pimples dotting my face, spiky afro sprouting out of my scalp.

***

Life in the shop was fun, until the court sessions dragged into months. Until we could no longer afford basic things. Until Mum began to lose weight.

Church members pleaded with Dad. Mum's family

members came to beg. Long-distance relatives from both sides held meetings. In the end, they said leaving our house at Sango would only be for a while. Dad would eventually change his mind and I could come around to see my father or sleep over whenever I wanted.

***

Sellers in the Bodija market advertised their wares with songs until their throats began to itch. They called buyers as though they might miss their way home.

There was a tree opposite our shop, and every night two bats sat on it, sometimes they hovered in the market. One night, I heard them talk like humans, and the voices sounded familiar.

The hoarse voice. The throaty laughter. They belonged to Mama Aisha's two friends.

Mama Aisha got lots of customers, not because she sold the best fabrics but because she was a nice and soft-spoken woman. She had a fashion sense that pulled eyes into a continuous stare whenever she walked by. She loved to buy food from Mum and, after eating, they would talk about business.

Mama Aisha punctuated every conversation with prayers.

May we sell today. May today bring us good fortune. May life not be hard for us.

The next morning Mama Aisha opened her store, and all she saw were ashes. No smoke. Bails of ash. No one could trace the source of the fire. Her two friends wailed more. They held her as she flailed like soft linen. They promised to be there through her struggles. I gave Mama Aisha's friends a piercing look.

If they knew I saw them on the tree, they did not show it.

***

While Mum mourned my brother, she neglected everyone. For days, she locked herself up in her room and went to the market barefoot, talking in a language no one understood. I thought she would die or lose her mind. After some months, she recovered but Dad had begun to see Bimpe's mother.

Mum channeled her frustration into her business. She worked hard, cooked and cleaned. She sent our sales girls away because she could no longer afford to pay them. She promised to re-employ them when she got back on her feet. At night I heard her muscles grumble. While asleep, her spirit walked the room picking up things, washing dishes and preparing meals.

The first day it happened, I believed she'd woken up early to prepare for the next day. I drifted back to sleep, but when morning came, she tapped me to go wash the dishes, and I knew then it was one of the visions.

Some days, I sat in the canteen listening to the voices of the wind, the sand, trees, and animals. Bodija is a hell of a place, everything talks. On other days, I spent the afternoon thinking about the new boy I had a crush on.

Everyone in my class had a yellow circle above their heads except the new boy, Vincent. His was bright red. His eyes shone like little stars. I was curious the day he walked into our class, the math teacher brought him. He rarely spoke except on the football field, where he shouted and ran like the wind. I loved to watch him.

I saw him enter Mama Aisha's store before it was burned; a woman wearing loads of gold jewelry held his hand, they came to buy fabric. And the day the store was burned, they both came to pay a condolence visit.

When he saw me, he entered our shop and complimented my outfit—khaki baggy shorts and a polo.

"You look different. I mean in a good way," he said.

The woman stood outside the shop looking at us.

"Thank you. Who is that woman? I asked.

"That is my mum. I guess it is time to go. See you in school."

The next day, he beamed and waved—he called my name

for the first time. We waved at each other every day till it transitioned into a friendship.

***

Aunty Bolaji, Mum's cousin who ran a booming restaurant in Lagos, taught Mum how to upscale her business. She was an innocent woman, I do not want to say dumb. She knew the ways of the world, she knew how to play the game but did not last in it.

The news of her death came on a Friday evening, regardless, Mum went to church for a vigil and dragged me along. She sat at the back of the church and wept. When we got home she told me to send messages to all her customers that we wouldn't be open for the week.

I imagined Aunty Bolaji's body in a coffin, red fingernails, braids running down her back to her butt, and large earrings. I tried not to think about her ample bosom; they were cut off, I was sure by a man who had sucked and cupped his hands around them during sex. Her naked mutilated body was found in front of her restaurant wrapped in a white duvet.

Before she died, Aunty Bolaji came to Ibadan and threw a party to celebrate the growth of Mum's business. She ordered the sales girls around and gave them instructions, gulped bottles and bottles of beer, till she got drunk.

"Hey, you." She pointed at me where I was doing dishes. "I am sure boys have started eating you now. Don't lie, ehn."

I was dumbstruck, scared that Mum would hear her silly joke and start to imagine things about me. But Mum was laughing heartily with customers who came to celebrate with us.

"You are not too young to do these things," Aunty Bolaji added, downing a cup of beer.

The vision was brief.

In it, she was wrapped in a bloody duvet. I was so shocked, one of the plates slipped and broke. I turned to look at her but she stared at me as if I were a crazy child.

"What do we call a woman who died without getting married or bearing children," I asked Mum after sending the text to our customers.

Her nose flared, she looked as though she would wring breath out of my nostrils.

"Even though Bolaji chose to enjoy the world as much as she wanted and decided to have no husband or child, she still deserves a befitting burial. Don't you ever ask me any silly question."

She handed me a list of things to buy in the market.

"You already know my customers. Tell them you want it just like I always buy it. Two baskets of tomato and pepper. A packet of Maggie." She made calculations and added extra money in case things had become more expensive.

I hated waving through the sweaty bodies in Bodija market. The noise hurt my ears. I walked the market with sleep still in my eyes.

I hated the vigil and the church—how the church boys stared at me as if my baggy jeans and shirt were a plaque. I hated the church because the girls reminded me of my failure at girlish things. I did not wear makeup, my bare face looked like the plain back of the hymn book. I always sat at the far end of the church, among boys and girls who were dragged to church by their devoted mothers. I stared at people who fell under the anointing, people who never left the church without creating a scene—sprawling, rolling and kicking the air as they prayed.

Mum always cried in church. She never spoke about Dad or the divorce; it seemed to me that she shoved them into a corner of her heart where they melted into tears during prayers.

***

The son of the pepper seller smiled anytime he saw me, but

I did my best to ignore him. His mother packed what I bought and I paid. But the son kept smiling as if he was hallucinating.

"Greet your mum for me, you hear."

I nodded in response.

"Do you ever talk?" the smiling son asked.

"My son likes you. Give him a chance, even though you don't even act like a girl."

It sounded like a privilege—something I did not deserve.

I felt a lump in my throat.

It was the right time to unleash the rage I had rammed for years, the rage that brewed inside me toward my father, his concubine and his daughter. The rage I had toward a world that made me feel like I would never be enough.

"Let the insane mother tell her filthy son that I don't need his love," I said. I did not care what they thought of me. I did not turn to look at them as I made my way to buy meat.

When I returned to the canteen, Mum was all about the burial preparations. She made calls and ordered the sales girls around. But I was locked up in my head, thinking about why I could do nothing about the visions. If I could not protect Aunty Bolaji, I needed to at least bring my parents back together.

***

The baby began to walk the day he turned one. Mum watched him from a corner of the living room where she was shelling melon seeds. I could see the rage in her eyes, the fury she had tamed for a whole year came loose.

As if he knew what his birth had done to her, the baby never went close to Mum.

I loved the boy, I doted on him. Mum did not state her displeasure in words, but she always found reasons to lash out at me whenever I played with him.

One Saturday, Mum did not go to her shop. She was down with a fever, lying on a mat in the living room. The baby held to the end of her cover cloth and Mum pulled with full force, sending him sprawling on the floor. He began to wail.

Bimpe and her mother came rushing from the kitchen.

"I know you never loved my son all this while. But tell me what a little boy could have done to deserve this hatred."

She held the child but he would not stop wailing.

Mum sat up quietly and began to pack up the mat.

"What exactly do you think you are doing? You want to kill my son like you killed yours?"

Mum dropped the mat, caught the blouse of the other woman and they were locked up in a tussle. When Dad came back, Bimpe's mum narrated everything that happened and added some extras to paint a more brutal scene.

"Mummy Lydia, why are you such a wicked woman. I will end up sending you out of this house and I mean it," Dad said.

"This house is mine too. We built it together. I don't know where you found the harlot you call a wife. She will never take my place."

"You must be out of your mind. Who is a harlot?"

Bimpe's mother ran in and another fight broke out.

***

Vincent stared at me vacantly. I could not tell him how I knew a question would be asked in an English test we had.

"When I saw the question, I remembered how you insisted we study it. You must be a witch," he said, pinching me. "How did you know?"

"I only guessed." I lied.

As he walked me to the shop after school, I caught furtive glances of him, lost in his head. We stood at the back of the canteen talking.

He inched closer and kissed me briefly.

I was shy but I wanted it to last longer. His lips were soft, there was a minty scent on his breath. He held my hand and told me he had to leave. I watched as he walked away, and for the first time, I noticed how muscular his frame was.

I repeated the scene in my head for the rest of the day, picturing it in different ways. What I would have done if I was not shy. What I would have told him. How I would have pressed my body against his, like they do in the movies. I prayed for it to happen again, and that I would be more prepared.

If Mum noticed my giddiness, she did not talk about it. When she counted the money we made, she sang hymns and created musical beats with her mouth. I slept, fantasizing about the kiss.

When I woke up, Mum was not on the bed. She was arranging pots and plates. I went back to sleep, thinking it was one of my morning visions.

I woke up again to see the sales girls sweeping the shop. 7:30 a.m. and Mum was nowhere in sight. School started at 8 a.m. We took our bath very early in the morning before people started to troop into the market. I could no longer take my bath. I washed my face and feet, put on my uniform and hurried to school.

After assembly, I saw Bimpe and Vincent giggling in our class corridor. I walked past them, pretending not to notice. I was furious. Vincent had probably done this with different girls in school.

Slowly, the day went by, stuck at my desk during break because I felt dirty and silly.

Vincent walked up to me as if nothing had happened.

"I did not know that girl is your sister."

"She is not my sister."

"But she lives with your father's wife. So?"

I was silent. He stared at his feet for a while.

"How come you never told me these things."

"I do not know."

"Well, I have something to tell you."

My heart leaped and my late-night thoughts rushed into my brain, blinding every sense of reason. I thought he wanted us to kiss again.

This will not be brief. I told myself.

He looked serious, a dark shadow forming around his eyes. "Do you know...what is his name? Ariyo. He is not your father's child?"

"How do you know?"

"I just know."

"Who told you?"

"Nobody, and I am sure you know."

"I do and I have plans, I just want it to be solid enough." On that day, I understood what the red circle above his head signified. Vincent was a seer too.

After school, we met Bimpe in her class, staring at the door as if she had been expecting us. We told her everything. Bimpe began to cry.

"I wanted to speak all this for a while but I thought no one would believe me."

We left school to go to my father's house, where Bimpe disclosed everything she knew.

Her mother sobbed silently—the baby sobbed too, as if he understood what was happening.

"Why are you not saying anything?" Dad asked.

Bimpe's mother knelt and begged, holding onto Dad's trousers.

He picked up his car key.

"If I find you in this house when I return, I will kill you."

***

I want to stay in the present. I do not want to talk about how Dad wore his shame elegantly. How he came to beg Mum under the guise of patronizing her business. And when she did not bulge, he brought relatives to beg on his behalf. And when she did not listen to them, he brought the pastor and church elders to beg on his behalf.

After two years, we were one family again, riding to

church in Dad's car. Mum's gele towered to the roof. For the third time, she asked Dad if her lipstick matched her skin tone.

SHINELLE L. ESPAILLAT

Virgo

Wind whipped the late-October leaves into a red-gold frenzy overhead, and Barbara tightened the belt on her trench coat without breaking stride as she walked toward the subway, the dying sunlight tinting her skin with bronze. She wished she had more time to enjoy the weather. She wasn't in a hurry—she never hurried—but time and the 5 train waited for no woman, and she had an appointment that she did not care to miss.

She took the stairs down to the dank darkness. Despite the cool air above, subway stations were always hot and damp, and this one was dimmer than usual, thanks to a couple of busted bulbs. She passed a group of teens, one of whom whistled at her. She shook her head and kept moving. Silly little boys couldn't even tell that she was old enough to be their mother. She took their noise as an attempt to return to normalcy. The trauma of September 11th still hung like a pall over New York, even as the city struggled to recover its voice. One of the boys shouted something obscene at her, but she let the words bounce off her back. Her sister would have called them a gang, but Barbara thought of them as harmless, happy to make themselves seem tough to their friends with language they were too young to really understand. Still, she walked far enough down the platform to lose their voices in the tunnel noise, and parked herself between a bent woman with an overflowing grocery cart and a young woman with her nose buried in a book. The young woman reminded Barbara of her niece, Kendra. Just that morning, Kendra had called to say that Barbara should visit, and Barbara had promised she would, made small talk and said nothing about tonight's appointment. She would decide after whether or not Kendra needed to know.

When the train came screeching to a halt, the young woman navigated the rush and dropped onto a seat without ever taking her eyes off the page. Barbara helped the old woman negotiate her cart over the gap, then grasped a strap and planted her feet. She almost never sat, even when seats were available. You couldn't tell how often they'd been cleaned, but you *did* know the kind of mess people got up to on them, and she would stand as long as she had strength to do so. She supposed it was silly, but it was something her mother had taught her, and the skin on the back of her thighs crawled at the thought of what might be crawling on those seats. Only when the train was in motion did she allow her thoughts to focus on the meeting that awaited her at the end of the ride. She assumed that whatever Angie had to say would ignite the fury that twenty years of absence had dimmed. She only hoped she could resist the urge to punch her sister in the face.

The train lurched and lumbered along, rocking the passengers like a rough cradle. The bent old woman, arms curled protectively around her cart, allowed herself to be lulled to sleep. Barbara could see a sheaf of greens peeking out of one of the bags, and imagined the woman going home to mix them with smoked neck bones, offer them as love to someone who would scarf them down without thanks, or tell her that she'd over-seasoned them. This was one reason among several why Barbara herself had never learned to cook. Why pour so much of yourself into something others could take and consume without care? Then she remembered Angie, cooking out of determined obligation rather than love. Was it obligation, finally, that had made Angie reach out and ask to meet? But Angie had abandoned obligation long ago, and whatever was compelling her now, it couldn't be love. *Love,* Barbara thought, sucking her teeth, *would have brought her back years ago.* Love should have kept her from leaving.

It was twilight, and raining, when they pulled into Dyre Ave, the conductor's heavy voice reminding them that this was the last stop, *last stop*, and that everyone needed to exit the train. The young woman snapped her book shut and tucked it under her arm, hurrying awkwardly into the deepening dark. Barbara felt around in her bag for her umbrella before she stepped onto the platform. It was always interesting to her that what was subway in Manhattan became an El in the Bronx. She thought her niece would say something profound about the aesthetics of economics. She wondered what Kendra would say if she knew that Angie was back. Was Angie back? Barbara rolled her eyes at herself. There was no point in speculating; she would just wait and see what Angie wanted. But she would cut her sister's throat, slice her from ear to ear, before she let Angie hurt Kendra again. She knew that much.

She also knew, she was sure, why Angie had asked to meet. The events of September 11th had spurred many a guilt-ridden reconciliation, and were probably the kind of cataclysmic force that would push Angie to end two decades of silence. Now, Barbara thought, Angie would want to come home, to be forgiven and to reclaim her place in the family. The question, whether Angie understood it or not, was whether or not Barbara would allow it.

She exited the station and squinted in the darkness, hoping she would see a gypsy cab pulling up to the corner. Instead, she saw the same group of boys, arranged in a circle around the young woman with the book. They weren't touching her, but every time she went to walk away, one of them would step into her path. Nobody else seemed to notice or care; certainly, the police officer standing at the station door stood silent and still. Barbara shook her head in disgust. The boys were laughing, jeering, pointing.

"Yo, she look like the troll under the bridge!"

"What's up with them coke bottles on her face? Look like

magnifying glasses!"

"Damn, shorty pay so much attention to them books she ain't pay attention to her hair!"

"Yo, you like studying so much; I got something you could study!" One of them grabbed his crotch and leered.

So unoriginal, Barbara thought as she walked over, raised her umbrella and popped the crotch grabber in the back of the head. She didn't bother telling them that they ought to be ashamed of themselves, that their mothers would be ashamed of them. She saw that they would not care. "Go home. Or go to the devil. But get on out of here."

The crotch grabber turned on her, holding the back of his head as though she'd really hurt him. She knew that she hadn't even raised a knot. She brought the umbrella down harder, right on his forehead, and he jumped back, clutching his head and cursing at her. The others got loud, but stood around, posturing but not making a move.

"Yo, why you buggin', old lady?"

"Young man. It's too bad nobody raised you right, but if you don't want me to break your head open, you all will go on, now. Go on." She didn't raise her voice. She didn't chase them. She didn't even make her face angry. She just stood, immovable, umbrella raised, shielding the young woman and staring them down, until they dissipated, mumbling about crazy bitches. The crotch grabber was still holding his head, and she wondered if maybe she'd hurt him more than she'd thought, but she could not afford to waver. She waited until they were too far to bother coming back before she lowered her umbrella and turned to the young woman.

"These boys and their testosterone. I hope they stay out of jail. Are you okay?"

The woman drew a shaky breath. "I guess." Her face trembled and sagged as she began to cry. "I have pepper spray in my bag, but I didn't think to use it."

Barbara saw a dark car slowly drift by on the other side of the street. She raised her arm to hail it, and the car executed a swift U-turn and stopped in front of them. "Here now. You're safe. Where are you headed? We better share this cab." She handed the young woman a tissue.

"I need to walk."

Barbara opened the door. "You need to get in this cab. I don't trust that those boys aren't waiting up the street."

The young woman peered fearfully in the direction the group had gone, then hopped into the car like a nervous rabbit. Barbara followed, closing the door firmly behind her. She prompted the woman to give her address, then followed up with the address Angie had provided. She sighed and shook her head.

"Those young fools. You're okay, though." She spoke in a soothing voice, the way she would to a toddler.

"I guess. They didn't actually hurt me or anything."

"Good. It's a damn shame." Only now did Barbara allow herself to feel the cocktail of shock, anger and fear. She had not supposed them to be dangerous. What did that say about her judgement? Of course, given where she was headed, who she was about to meet, her judgement was faulty anyway. Angie was as dangerous, in her own way, as that group of boys, and you couldn't scare her off with an umbrella. Still, Barbara believed herself equal to the challenge. She had to be.

"Thank you. I should have said it earlier. I don't know what I would have done if you hadn't been there."

"You would have thought of something. You know what they say. God looks out for fools and babies."

The woman stopped dabbing at her eyes with the already-damp tissue and looked confused. "Which one am I?"

Barbara chuckled. "I don't think you're a fool. Don't tell me how old you are." She held up a hand to stop the flood of information the woman was clearly about to share. She thought it best to distract the young woman, keep her from focusing on what had possibly been a closer call than she'd realized. "You'll only make me feel like a relic. But do tell me about what you're reading."

The request shot the woman full of energy. She kept up a steady stream of chatter about the characters and the world inside that book, calmer and more sure of herself, moving past the tears and shakiness, so that she seemed quite at ease by the time the cab stopped at the address she'd given. She got out of the cab, but held the door when Barbara would have closed it.

"I can't thank you enough. You really are like a guardian angel."

"You stay safe." Barbara smiled.

The woman reminded her even more of Kendra, which of course reminded her of Angie, which raised Barbara's hackles more than the gang of boys had. No matter what arguments Angie marshaled, Barbara was determined to serve as guardian or avenger tonight.

By the time the cab pulled up in front of the address, it was full on dark and full-on raining, but Barbara didn't mind. She stood on the broken pavement in front of the little house, letting the rain pool around her boots, though she made sure the umbrella covered her hair. The porch light was on, highlighting the neat garden and hedges. Barbara wondered whose house this was, and how long Angie had been there. Maybe she'd been hiding five miles away from them all this time. Her thoughts and pulse kept pace with the downpour. The pristine picture she had in her mind of the sister she used to know could not possibly match the person inside the house. Would she be gnarled, shriveled and hideous, like a reverse Dorian Gray? Would she weep for what she'd done? Would she say that she, too, had spent long stretches of time probing the sister-void in her soul, like poking a tongue into the space of a freshly extracted wisdom tooth?

None of that mattered, Barbara reminded herself, straightening her spine and placing a firm lid on the surge of emotion. She walked slowly up the path, clinging to the phantom feeling of the autumn sun on her face, of her sense of purpose and assuredness as she strode through the world, of the strength that allowed her to face down a gang of teenage ruffians with nothing more than fabric and flexible wire.

She raised a hand to ring the bell, but the door opened before she could press it.

She and Angie stared at each other for a moment.

Barbara felt as though she'd dropped her umbrella and the sky had poured pails of cold water over her freshly-pressed hair. She pressed her lips together. Angie opened hers.

"Hello, sister. Come on in out of the rain."

Barbara allowed herself the space between lightning and thunder to take in the reality. Angie was there, alive and in the flesh, for the first time in two decades. The years had not punished her, physically, anyway; there were no bitter, hard lines around her eyes or mouth, no widening of her frame, and whoever she paid to dye the grays was doing a good job. A bitter crust of resentment settled over Barbara's skin as she stepped over the threshold without returning the greeting. Angie didn't even seem sorry.

Angie closed the door. "You used to be more polite," she said, as she reached out a hand for Barbara's things.

"You used to matter." Barbara shrugged out of her coat and handed off the umbrella, both of which Angie hung neatly on a spindly rack, giving no indication that she'd felt the insult.

"Take off your boots, please. These aren't my floors." She waited for Barbara to comply, then led the way to a living room filled with overstuffed, plastic-covered furniture. "This is my friend's great-aunt's house. These old women and their plastic covers. This stuff and twinkies will outlast a nuclear bomb. Do you remember when Ma wanted—"

"Ma's dead. She's been dead for years. She died wishing she could see you again."

Barbara stayed on her feet. She admitted to herself that she'd been harsh in delivering the news, that she'd wanted to wound. She could do more damage still—there was harder news to share—but the specter of their mother, frail, confused and longing for her lost girl, made Barbara hesitate. She could all but hear their mother's voice, firm and cautioning. *God don't like ugly.* She crossed her arms and tapped her socked foot on the hardwood, softening her voice just a little. "What is it that you want, Angie? Why are you here?"

Angie slapped a hand against a wall, and the living room was filled with light. She crossed the room and dropped into a fat recliner, crackling and squeaking against the plastic cover as she did. She rested her hands on her thighs, and looked down at them. "Ma's dead." Her tone was as calm and even as Barbara's had been against the gang of boys. "When did she die? How?"

This stoicism irritated Barbara, and she sucked her teeth. "What did you think, that we would all stay exactly the same as when you left, like we were flash frozen? We're not fossils, Angie. We are all flesh and blood." She didn't move, except to breathe. "What is it that you want?"

Angie raised her head, and in the brighter living room light, Barbara could see that she'd been wrong; Angie had changed, but only her eyes. Twenty years ago, they'd been impatient and critical; now her eyes were hungry. *Good*, Barbara thought. She hoped that Angie had been starvingly lonely.

Angie's hands curled into fists, then uncurled and curled again, knotting the fabric of her pants. She ground her lips together, and Barbara could all but hear the clenching of her jaw. When she spoke, she sounded as though she'd been swallowing shards of her own teeth. "I had to leave. Once I'd made up my mind that it was time, I had to go. You know that. But I want to see them. I need to. Just once, to tell my side of it."

"But you did tell." Barbara still did not move. "I have your letter—the one letter you ever wrote—and I let Kendra read it, so there you go. Your story is told." She should have known that Angie's motive would be selfish: to tell, to be heard, to be understood. But her conscience snagged a little. *To see them*, Angie had said. *Them*. She didn't know. The worst truth pressed against her teeth, weighed on her tongue, and now she wished that she did not have to be the one to tell Angie that she had waited too long to make her big comeback. She had left two children behind, but only one remained.

Barbara watched Angie grapple with the truth she had already received. *The hunger in her eyes must*, Barbara thought, *be a symptom of deeper change, like rot in wood*. The sister Barbara remembered would have fired back against every rudeness Barbara had leveled, would have wielded anger like a whip and shredded anyone who talked to her that way. The old Angie would have demanded to see her children and told Barbara off six ways from Sunday for breaking the news of their mother's death so casually. But then, the old Angie would have been there to witness it for herself.

Barbara sat now on the sofa, crackling against the hard plastic. She kept her spine straight, treating the furniture as she would a seat on the train. She didn't trust this new, rotted sister. But the sight of her, curved and weakened, called out the instinct that had made Barbara both sword and shield earlier. She sighed, and softened her tone a few degrees more.

"Why now?" She allowed the old curiosity to unwind like a river inside her.

Angie shook her head. "That's not important."

"You don't get to decide what's important. You are not in charge."

"I see you've grown a little bit of spine since I left."

So, Angie still had a few sharp edges left. Though she kept her expression unimpressed, Barbara was glad of it. She could recognize, and knew how to handle, an Angie bordered by hard angles better than she could this pulpy-centered imposter wearing her sister's skin.

"Let's stop dancing around this. Plain facts: you left us all, without hesitation or reservation, without any shred of remorse, so I know you're not looking for sympathy. You left those kids for the rest of us to raise, and I notice you didn't call their father or anyone else. You could have gone straight to Kendra, but you didn't. You came to me. So yes, I am in charge, and yes, I decide what's important. I ask the questions. And if I don't like the answers, I will walk out of here the same way you did: without hesitation or reservation. And that'll be the end of it."

She could see Angie run her tongue over her teeth, not liking the flavor of the conversation. She could see Angie searching for a way to gain the upper hand, even now, with no foundation for rightness and no premise for winning. She watched the rot fail to prop up the hard shell, and Angie folded in on herself like wet, hollow bark.

"Okay then. It's nothing dramatic. I'm in a book club." She twisted her mouth into a sad grin. "I'm in a book club, and somebody put Kendra's book on the list for next month. I just about collapsed when they brought up the name. Kendra Burke. I thought, 'well maybe it's another Kendra Burke. It's not that unique of a name." She stared blankly at a spot on the wall as she spoke, partially, Barbara supposed, lost in memory. "That's what Marcus said when I was pregnant with her. Wanted to call her Marcusette or some nonsense. She ought to be glad I put my damn foot down on that one." She rubbed an absent hand over her flat belly. Barbara wondered if she were reliving phantom kicks, or if she just remembered how much she'd hated her pregnant body. "But I went and got the book, and there was her face on the back. Not the clingy little girl I knew, but this grown-ass woman. And I thought, 'she did it.' She is extraordinary. She is excellent."

Barbara did not care for the look of pride settling on

Angie's face. "*Despite* you. Not because of you. You don't get to take any credit for who she's become."

"Don't I? She had to shape herself around my not being there. Even my absence helped create her."

Crossing her arms and legs, Barbara brushed aside Angie's arrogance, even though part of her accepted that truth.

"So, you saw her book and decided to come rushing back. Fame made her worth your time."

Kendra was not famous. One book of poetry, even when moderately well-received, did not necessarily make a person famous, though Barbara had felt as much pride as if she'd written it herself, and browbeaten half her office into buying copies.

"That's not it. It was just, seeing her face out of the blue like that, seeing her name. I couldn't pretend that they weren't out there in the world anymore. I couldn't make myself forget. And then I started to wonder what else she'd done with her life, and what Max was doing, and I just...missed them. Hard. So hard it was unbearable."

Barbara nodded in mock empathy. "Oh, I know. So hard it was unbearable. You know, that's just how Kendra felt about it, when you left. She missed you so hard she could not bear it. Max, maybe not so much. He was so little." She rocked a little, to lull the keening sorrow she felt whenever she thought about Max. "But then, you know, the oddest thing happened. Life kept moving. And one day passed, and then the next, and then the next. And funny enough, what happened was that she *did* bear it. She survived you. So, I think she can continue to manage quite nicely without you now."

Pride lifted Angie's chin. "Of course, she can. I read that book. I know she's strong. It's me." She wilted, sagging into soft folds. "I'm the one. I'm the one who's weak and needy now."

The sisters stared across the room at each other, each lost

in her own thoughts, so that the only sound was the crackle of plastic settling beneath them.

Barbara did not believe that just seeing Kendra's name in print would be enough to make Angie regret twenty years of silence. Something else was driving that hunger. When it clicked, Barbara gasped, closed her eyes and sank deeper, so that her back pushed against the cover. "Oh. I see. You're dying."

Angie twitched as though a fly buzzed in her ear. "Don't be so dramatic."

Barbara almost laughed. "You've basically come back from the dead--because you're dying, no less--but you're calling me dramatic." She did laugh, then. "Irony, indeed."

"Laughter seems inappropriate." Angie crossed her arms and glared, though her trembling chin spoiled the effect.

"Oh, I think it's appropriate." Barbara leaned forward for emphasis. "I think it's exactly the right response. I think that even if your heart leapt out of your chest right now. I would laugh. And I still wouldn't let you see Kendra."

"I came to you as a courtesy. I don't actually need your permission."

"You came to me," Barbara settled deeper into the plastic, her voice calmer as she grasped further truth, "because you were scared that no one else would see you. You wanted me to pave the way for you. You didn't care about seeing me, you didn't miss your little sister any more than you missed your kids." The old wound throbbed, like the echo of a sprained ankle. Her big sister didn't love her. She shook her head. "Still the same, selfish Angie."

"I was a good mother, when I was there." The mulish set of Angie's jaw was painfully familiar. "I just didn't have enough left to give them and still be me. I wouldn't expect you to understand."

A flicker of doubt cast a shadow over Barbara's resolve. Maybe there was more than Angie had expressed in the one letter, something that Kendra needed to hear. "All right then.

Make me understand. Tell me your story."

Angie licked her lips. "I wanted to tell Kendra—"

Barbara held up a hand. "Tell me." She allowed herself, one more time, to want to know what would make someone choose to stop mothering.

A spasm of mutinous anger contracted Angie's brow. Barbara could imagine how hard it must be, taking orders when you used to be the boss, but she would not yield. She sat stone still, a sphinx who had offered the riddle: what could Angie say that would make any difference? When she spoke, the words were an eruption.

"It was killing me! Every day, every year, every stage—all of it. The breastfeeding when I didn't want to be touched at all, the reviewing sight words when I wanted to read my own books, the rushing home to bathe and feed them when I wanted to stay at work and excel. Forcing myself to coddle, to coach, to push them to be their best, when I couldn't ever be my own best, when I never wanted to do any of it at all!" She paused, panting, and stared down at the clenched fists pressed against her stomach. She waited until her breathing was even before she continued. "I had to choose me. My *self* was dying." Sadness, and a hint of scorn, tinged her gaze as she met Barbara's eyes again. "You wouldn't get it. You never had kids; you never had to give up your whole self that way."

There was nothing so different in Angie's words now than there had been in the letter, except that hearing the anguish hurt Barbara more than reading it had done. But she couldn't afford to show sympathy or any emotion that Angie would use as a fulcrum to pry open a portal for reentry. Instead, she challenged Angie's presumption.

"How do you know?"

A wave of uncertainty flowed over Angie's face. "I...I just assumed. You never wanted kids. I—did you?"

Barbara snorted. "The first question you ask me about me is just as self-serving as everything else you've said and done."

She rose to her feet. Angie rose with her, crossed the room and rested a callused hand on Barbara's arm. The long fingers, with the short, neat nails were just like her daughter's. Barbara wavered for just a moment, wondering if she should let Kendra, who was after all a grown woman now, decide for herself. But she'd fought so hard for so long to escape the shroud of her mother's memory that Barbara was loath to disinter this skeleton.

"I did miss you." Angie's face contorted itself into a shape that Barbara had never seen on it before. It took a moment to recognize it as contrition. "It's not just because I'm sick. And you're right. I am sick. I am...I haven't even said the word. I won't say it now. But I missed you. Every day. I wanted to call you a thousand times. Leaving you alone was my punishment for leaving them alone. Please. I am asking you. Let me see them."

Barbara placed her hand over her sister's and squeezed. She would not say it aloud, but part of her—the part that never had children and never wanted to—understood why Angie had left. The million decisions, great and small, that went into keeping a little person alive, could overwhelm you so that you disappeared beneath them. And even then, even when you'd made all the decisions and thought all was well, the world could snatch them, quick as a crocodile, and you'd be left with nothing but old clothes and sorrow. It was too much.

She could lean into that understanding. She could open her arms and enfold Angie; she could fill in the concave sister hole that twenty years of time had not fully healed. But she realized that she had been asking herself a question that Angie had never asked: *what would Kendra want?* Kendra, who did not deserve to have her own healed wounds ripped open.

The flicker of doubt sputtered out, leaving the grey ash of choice. Barbara allowed herself one moment to feel a well of love, to mourn anew her loss, before she turned to serve as shield once more. But now, she decided, she would shield her sister as well.

She was tender, gentle as she removed Angie's hand from her arm. She ignored Angie's pleas as she stepped into her boots and zipped them. She tied her trench coat and closed the door on Angie's choking sobs. She would allow Angie to die without knowing that she'd outlived one of her children, and she would protect Kendra from the last of Angie's selfishness.

Confident, composed, and utterly heartbroken, Barbara raised her umbrella and strode into the cool autumn night.

SABINE WILSON-PATRICK

Ocean Belly

The woman who waxed my legs walked into the ocean last week. My mother told me so. I think she just died, the bells tolled like she died. Anyways, I miss her. She gave me tips on how to be a real woman. How to put crushed hibiscus in the trash every month to cover the scent of blood. Marked my legs with chalk where my skirts should fall, another mark for where to tug it up for discounted coconut bread. She was sharp and pointed like a weapon. I do her job now. Not waxing legs. When the cars start rolling down the hill, I sit on a bench by the water and haul fishing nets up out of the surf. They are empty. The mackerel comes in a big truck in the night. You can't even catch them off this beach, but that doesn't really matter. I haul in imaginary fish until the sun is hovering over my head, for lunch I have to eat something I could have pulled out of a tree. I rub tamarind over my gums and pretend it's cocaine. After lunch I run helter skelter down the dusty cart roads with the other village children in their summer clothes. We don't like each other. Somebody has fucked someone else's boyfriend, someone else called the other's mother loose. We pretend to play tag, or some African game that involves a soft ball and chanting. On rare occasions we put on impromptu stick fighting exhibitions. But I don't do those anymore. I hit Caiel in the eye with a river tamarind branch and his mother told the congregation I was possessed by the devil. I am not. After the sun goes down and the tourists are gone the children collect their phones from their respective woven drawstring sacks, and families listen to the news on the radio. I drifted out into the cane fields and snuck cigarettes, my ash lighting up the night as a Cyclops' eye. Or some other wicked thing. In a way, I was happy she died. I preferred her job to the one I had before. Fashioning cowrie shells into earrings and wind chimes. All her responsibility had been hypothetical, no one expected her to catch fish that weren't there.

I settled into routine. Peeled mangoes with chunks of obsidian and my teeth. Occasionally, I would shout something guttural and incoherent to Mr. Delancey as he hacked apart coconuts and sold $10 metal straws to drink the water. I sat on my smooth, hot stone, baking on the sun. Hauling my fish. Ade stretched out next to me. She always reminded me of something precious and made of glass. Ade didn't have a real job, she was an ornament. She pressed her body up against the main road and twisted oily fingers through her forest of sister locs. They jingled with filigree covered cuffs and pebbles painted to look like pearls, all vying for a spot around her hips. The pastor's wife hung heavy silks off her square shoulders to make her look more feminine. She looked like a rare bird. People stopped to take photographs of her, asked her how she'd grown her hair so long. Braid fistfuls of it, grazing her skin. Paper dipping into ink. She was a tourist attraction, in every sense of the word. I think if the pastor's wife wasn't so consumed by thoughts of holiness, she would let them fuck Ade for pennies on the dollar.

"What do your imaginary fish look like?" she asked, gazing at her mottled reflection in the water.

"I don't know...rainbow-colored and shimmery like in that book your mother used to read us when we were kids."

"We are kids."

"10 years ago, when we were actually children. The damn fish that gave away all his pretty scales," I snapped, gathering armfuls of my net to cast again.

When Ade looked at me, I always forgot what I'd been thinking before. She had sad eyes the size of fried eggs, and smoker's lips that looked like cut peaches. All of my adolescence was spent stealing glances at her, or just blatantly staring.

"What's your problem, Elijah? You seem angry," she finally said, sitting up to stare back at me.

"I thought counseling was Mama Asha's job, not yours."

"Is your problem spiritual in nature?"

"No." When we were children, I told Ade everything. Pieces of pottery I broke and crushed up into sand, the boys at church who made my stomach clench. I never stopped, I just stopped having things to tell her. "Look, only because you asked, but it's about Kwame."

She immediately perked up, intrigued,

"I thought he really liked me, I think he really likes me, and I just let it go too far, okay? Which I know is my fault and I don't really have a right to have-"

"Kwame...like Mama Kaya's son?"

"Yes."

"And what happened?"

I cast my net back into the water, I'd just been waiting to disrupt its stillness, to send ripples all the way to Africa.

"Nothing," I said, trying too hard to make it sound unimportant. I didn't want Ade to think I was in love; he was a stupid man to love. Ade thought all men were stupid to love, she'd loved Jacki before she walked into the ocean.

"Was it good? ...was it big?"

"Yes, I think, I don't know, I have nothing to compare it to. And I'm not telling you if it was big, I wouldn't want him to tell his friends about me."

"Well, could he even really see you?"

I fucked him in the cane fields, nestled between the night's nicotine. All that he knew about my body was its softness. He whispered that my skin felt like I'd just come from the ocean, cold and slick and welcoming. Holding fistfuls of my hair he said it felt like nothing, like clouds. His mother was a potter and his father was a drummer, he wasn't born into a way with words. I told him that his hands were rough like cat's tongues, but he held me tighter anyways. So tight I could feel his heart hammering away in his chest. It was the only way I knew he was there in the dark of the night.

"Nobody could see us, that was kind of the point. It was a little while ago, and I haven't seen him since, and I miss him and I feel foolish for missing him and foolish for being with him like that and foolish for telling you about it."

"Instead of feeling so very foolish, which you are not, you should just go see him. What does he do now?"

Men in town weren't ornamental like Ade, or local color like me. White women felt threatened by Black men swinging their arms in the street. Instead, when they got to be around Kwame's age, they crawled out of the primordial soup that was our village and went to work real jobs. They became construction men, bootblacks, bus drivers, and children who stopped coming home. Kwame cleaned windows and frames at an art gallery in the city. He would come back suddenly and briefly with pockets full of postcards of art that had been on exhibit. Or little thimbles full of powder I could turn into paint with my spit.

"He's gone, Ade. Gone far."

"Don't you think he'll come back soon? Maybe you could call him?"

"No, I don't know that he would pick up."

***

I came home smelling of ocean spray and Ade's shea butter lip sheen. I wanted to stay out with her all night, but I wasn't so old that my mother could not call me in off the street from a mile away. It was just us in the house that swayed in the wind. The photos of dead relatives rattled on the walls when I walked. My father gazed down disapprovingly, no doubt thinking what a willful child he had produced, my grandmothers and grandfathers agreed. My older sister would have argued that I was spirited. The trinkets rumbled too.

Little wood carvings of nurse sharks resting their shoveled heads on the mantle, crude clay figurines of slave women with big behinds and headwraps, porcelain ones of white women with parasols and petticoats. Most, if not all, were gifts that tourists had given my mother for healing what ailed them. My mother's gifts lay in her ability to brew bush tea that didn't taste like bush tea. *It cleans the blood,* she would tell me, grinding ginger in the mortar. I would pick stalks of different vines in the brush and ask her if she could make tea that would make my boobs bigger. *Bush tea is no match for time,* she would say.

The dining room table was littered with small civilizations of letters. Many opened, some closed. Fat manila envelopes always contained photographs or scans. Blank brain scans with lengthy paragraphs about how my mother must be God. I think she started to believe them, I think she believed that there were real fish in my net.

"You have got to stop hanging out with Miss Moore's girl. Every day it feels like I call you in before the witching hour," my mother remarked as I rounded the narrow corner to the kitchen. She was frying escovitch in the cast iron. It was staring at me. I stared back at it. My mother covered its eyes with scotch bonnets like she was putting in the rest. I winced.

"Just because I am spending time with Ade doesn't mean I'm going to get like her," I replied, knowing exactly what my mother was thinking.

She sucked her teeth at me. She sucked her teeth at the escovitch. "All I know is if I have to call you in again I'm going to tell Mama Asha you have the devil in you again."

"How does hitting a boy with a stick equate to the devil in me? Because nobody ever explained."

"Elijah, the devil is the devil is the devil," she cautioned, waving her spatula at me wildly. She splattered the cream colored walls with hot oil, still mumbling her mantra under her breath.

My mother's fear of the devil came from her youth. Her

and my father had Dayo young. They didn't mean to have her. It was before my father was even old enough to move away from home, the two of them worked the same job. They would dress up in their summer clothes and he would chase her all the way up out of the valley to the main road, a long arm reaching out from the village. It drew in tourists, they wondered where these feral children came from, shaking shell studded cowbells and dripping with salt water. It didn't take them long to hollow out pieces of the lonely world over cliffs that fenced them in. My mother never told me how my father felt about Dayo. Just that they got married in a little ceremony in the church and the village buzzed with how in love they seemed. I liked to believe they were deeply in love but all they were was young.

She got older when Dayo walked into the sea. They wanted me to come out looking like her but I didn't. Something rounded out my face and my eyes and my mother would tut tut tut her tongue and say that I was made of raindrops. Dayo was the cliff at the end of the valley.

***

Mr. Delancey had run out of metal straws. I watched a white woman in her twenties press her lips to the hole he gouged in the coconut and drink. It was vaguely erotic. More so when she slid the $20 into his hand and smiled wistfully. Five hired cars had parked haphazardly on the side of the gravel road. The dust they kicked up in the air hung there, it was such a still day. A father and his three daughters took out their phones to capture every inch. The pink and yellow and green houses perched precariously on their mahogany legs, the palm frond thatch roofing that camouflaged sturdy galvanized steel. Wood whittled into sea turtles, cowrie shells rattling in heart shaped windchimes. The smallest girl ran up to a stall with miniature versions of the houses made out of driftwood. Delicate and exploitatively priced. Her sister asked if they could get fried fish. A group of men from a hired Land Rover paced around the village laughing. Perhaps about the primitiveness of it all, perhaps about one of them gazing at a woman bathing by the standpipe. Everybody could tell he wanted to be soaking wet with her.

I waded waist deep into the ocean, letting the net and my bundled cotton skirts float and encircle me on the surface. I liked to watch the visitors. Count the fistfuls of money they turned over in exchange for small pieces of the old world. I dreamt of charging them for hunks of rock cut out of the cliffside.

"Excuse me. English?" One of the men was looking down on me from the rock I sat on to fish. Against the sun, he looked like a messiah, but as he bent down to talk to me he looked perfectly ordinary. His face was made gentle by narrow, downturned eyes, like he was wanting to be forgiven for something. Everything about him was tugging him into the earth, his heavy jaw and his hollow cheeks and his sloping shoulders. He looked so very petulant. "English?" he said again.

"My name is Elijah, not English," I replied, trying my very best to tease the accent out of my words.

He laughed.

"I'm sorry, um, my name is Solomon." He left his accent. He sounded British, but I always thought they sounded British.

"Solomon as in he who built the temple?"

"What?"

"King Solomon. From the Bible."

"I mean, I can be your king, love," he smirked. The men always smirked, but never at me.

"You're funny, Solomon. What do you want from me?"

"Nothing really, I was just curious about what you catch in these waters."

The devil, I thought. "Nothing at all today."

"Do you think all the commotion scared them off? I

imagine you don't get that many visitors coming somewhere so remote."

I let the current carry me forward until I was inches away from him, perched on the rocks. I felt like a mermaid, mythically beautiful and soaking wet.

"I wish we had more visitors, it's so lonely. So far away from whatever else is out there." I sighed, putting on my best look of wide-eyed wistfulness.

He didn't want anything I could give him, he talked to me until the receding tide left my sopping skirt clinging to my thighs. He told me about his job, his ugly little traumas, the tamarind I was rubbing on my gums and highs that didn't come from cane sugar. I knew that his mother loved him but didn't like him, that one of his friends jumped off a cliff into the Atlantic, how he paid his way into his Law School and fucked his professor. Armfuls of things I didn't need to know. I didn't so care what he said, I was simply mesmerized. Watching his lips curl and press against his teeth as he smiled down at me. The ocean breeze could take skin off the bone but he never stopped smelling of weed smoke and antibacterial soap. He promised he would come back again, but I didn't believe him.

The sun was coming down the west when Ade came swanning over to me. She looked godly too. I wondered if this was how I must have looked to Solomon, so black I could be alien, so black I could be God. She asked me about him and I had nothing to say.

"I think Kwame would be jealous," she joked.

"Why? I'm not his wife."

"Would you want to be?"

"Want to be what?"

"His wife?" I paused, imagined myself standing at the altar where I took communion and lit candles in my youth. The painted black figurine of Jesus leering at me from his lofty position on the cross, my mother stabbing my scalp with hair pins, being cocooned in layers and layers of coarse linen for him to peel back and consume me.

"Of course I would," I finally replied.

I waited for her to call me a liar, but she just started to tell me about how she had imagined marrying Jacki. She always said they would run away, go south all the way to the edge of the island. All the way to the edge of the world. She asked me if I would come south with her instead.

***

Every Sunday before worship, my mother scrubbed across my cheeks with a scouring pad. She told me it made me look prettier. I would spend every Sunday at worship holding my cold hymn book to my swollen cheeks. I sang from memory; we all sang from memory. Every Sunday we would filter out of our houses in the somber procession to the decrepit church on the main road. The mothers all suffocated beneath uniform wool skirts, their daughters bound their chests with tight linen wraps secured over their bony shoulders. Every Sunday the sermon would feature a tangent on the sanctity of the body. The purity of the flesh.

"First Corinthians 7:9 says of sex 'if they cannot exercise self-control, they should marry. For it is better to marry than to burn with passion.' This is the word of our Lord," Pastor Bellamy's dick pressed up against his pants. Ade looked across the aisle at me knowingly. When we got home my mother broke a wooden spoon against my open palms, her nuclear deterrent.

Nobody worked on Sunday, after church the street became very silent. My mother mostly spent the day wandering through the brush, collecting pockets full of herbs. Ade repented. I drifted through the village like sahara dust in the summertime. Solomon was waiting for me at the bottom of the hill. I wasn't expecting him.

"Didn't I say I would come back?"

"I figured that's just what you say, not what you'd actually do." Heat rushed to my raw cheeks.

"Yeah well I'm a nice guy like that. Don't you know any nice guys?"

"Nothing happens in the village on Sunday, there's not much to see," I deflected.

He propped up against his rental car and asked me to come away with him for a day.

I'd been in a car a handful of times. Once when my father died, and again when my mother's bush tea could not stop my seizures. I couldn't blame him for treating me like I was primitive, but he thought I had just discovered fire. He ripped apart a Marlboro Gold and rubbed the tobacco into my palms, tried to teach me how to breathe deep enough for it to hurt just a little. We drove further and further down the coast. It was lonely everywhere, not just home, but it was comforting loneliness. Just me and him, watching the road fall away in chunks behind us. The spindly grove of river tamarind gave way to low hanging bearded fig trees that clothed the road in an emerald-colored darkness for miles. Solomon didn't have as much to say to me. Snippets of thoughts, he asked me if I thought he was handsome, told me he thought I was pretty. His hands were soft and cold, the half moons of his nails left imprints on my thigh. We pulled over under the shade of the trees.

"Can I ask you something.?"

"Yes."

His cold, soft hands were becoming a little clammy, "Have you ever fucked before?"

"Yes."

"Have you ever fucked a white guy?"

"No."

"I think you'd like it."

"I think I'd like a cigarette."

Without waiting for permission, I pulled out the Marlboro

flipped upside down in the pack and stepped out of the car to smoke. He leaned beside me on the hood of the car.

"I'm serious," he insisted, "I've never had any complaints."

Somehow, his downturned eyes looked sadder than they ever had before, I thought they might just slide off his face and into a puddle on the asphalt. When he kissed me, he bit my lip like he was trying to draw blood. Eventually he did; his tongue tasted like iron and tar. His clammy hands left prints on the skin of my shoulders and back, my cheek left prints on the pewter paint job of his rental. He told me that I had a great body; he held on tight like he was afraid I would slip away.

***

I steeped four months' worth of unused hibiscus into tea; I prayed for blood that never came again. My mother used a Bible this time, it wouldn't break against my skin. She wished it would. The kettle never stopped singing, she force-fed me mugwort tea and white rum until I couldn't breathe. It didn't work. She wished it would.

She started Sunday morning with a mouthful of bobby pins, twisting and curling my thicket of hair into something dignified. Ade studded the bun with shells and painted rocks. They wrapped my stomach tightly with yards of linen and draped it over my shoulders.

Kwame stood at the altar unflinching. Made of stone. We had spent our childhoods being subjugated right there, under the watchful gaze of God. And right there we weren't children anymore. I wasn't a child as we walked back down the aisle side by side, I wasn't a child as he reluctantly took my hand and held it tight. I wasn't a child as he slid my many skins off of my shoulder and saw my body in the daylight. He seemed so sure. He had always wanted a son.

***

Kwame painted the walls of the house he built for us. He wanted his son's room to be white so it would stay cool; I painted yellow petals on the ceiling so the baby would have something to unknowingly gaze at. Instead of blood I prayed for Blackness.

"Did you think of a name yet?" Ade asked me one day.

"No. I told Kwame he can name it."

"It? Don't call the child an 'it', Elijah, you'll give him a complex."

"We don't know that it's a he," I argued back. "We could have a girl."

"The Gidharis only have sons, for generations, nothing but sons, you better hope it's a son," I couldn't tell if she was joking. Ade had a way of knowing things I'd never told her.

"Kwame likes the name Nael, it means gift from God."

"Is it?"

"Is it what?"

"A gift from God?"

***

My mother told me that the first time she held me I felt worth it. Worth all the pain.

The first time I held my daughter, she felt like she was worth her weight in ashes. Her skin looked like sand, I pulled my fingers effortlessly through little tufts of soft curls. She had big black eyes like seeds, but they were downturned. Sad eyes.

I named her Asiel, made by God, and thought of Solomon, pressed against the sun like a deity. It's normal for her to be pale, I promised every visitor to our house, like I was trying to convince myself. Someone else took my place hauling in imaginary fish. Kwame fired pots in his mother's studio and stretched animal hide for his father's drums. My mother told me I should start working on a craft so that I could help provide for my daughter. She suggested wood carving; I took notches out of my fingers and thumbs. She suggested sewing; I stitched my skin to cotton. Finally, I settled on painting. Over that month I captured everything I could: The beech trees bending in the window, tropical storms rolling in off the Atlantic, Ade standing alone in the street, my husband and my daughter looking at each other like strangers.

I whiled away the extra hours trying to bake my daughter in the sun. She liked the waves, the wet sand. She wanted to consume every part of the shore she could fit in her tiny little mouth, she screamed when she realized she couldn't swallow the ocean.

Each Sunday, I put her in the same dress. It was coarse white cotton, decorated with spots of blood from needle bites. Pastor Bellamy's voice calmed her. She would uncomprehendingly coo at his notions of sanctity and love, grasping the hymn book in her fat little hands. Each Sunday the women at church whispered that she wasn't getting any darker. She didn't have anything of mine to defend herself, her eyes melted down her cheeks, her heavy jaw was always wet. Each Sunday the hot lump of shame grew in my throat. In the night I would squeeze her face in my hands and will it to be round. I mopped up her features to no avail.

Kwame stopped looking at her, Kwame stopped looking at me. I painted close-ups of the lines in his face as they deepened. White paint piled up; I never painted his smile.

My daughter babbled at me as I picked her up that Sunday night and held her to my chest.

"You can't take her with you to go have a cigarette," Kwame said, stopping me at the door.

"I'm not, I told you I quit."

"You told me a lot of things, Elijah."

"...she's restless, I'm taking her for a walk."

He let me pass.

The village at night was the loneliest it ever was, but it wasn't quiet. You could hear the distant hum of radios, river tamarind being tugged against the wind, waves combing through the sand. It would have been comforting. My daughter was comforted, she reached out to the stars. I wanted to give them to her. But there was nothing I could give to her. She would have to burn down the village to feel its warmth.

I sat with her on the stone I thought I would spend my entire youth on. I sat there, running my thumb over her chin.

"This is where your mama worked before...before she met your father. I used to fish. And I would catch the most beautiful fish, with rainbow-colored scales that sparkled in the sun. They were so pretty. And everybody from miles around would come to see the fish your mama caught. And that's how I met your father, babygirl. He thought the fish I caught were so beautiful, and he thought I was beautiful too. And I had all these dreams with him, about running away together and seeing the world. Because we were just so in love. We were so so in love. But he had to go back to where he came from, and so Mama had to find someone she loved just as much who would love you just as much. And that's when she got married to your papa, who loves her so so much too. Your papa loves you so so much, but he's confused. He doesn't understand why God gave us a baby who doesn't look anything like Mama and Papa. And I keep...I keep promising that when you're a big strong girl, you'll look just like us."

I waded waist deep into the water with my baby, "but I don't think that's going to happen, babygirl, I don't think it can. And I don't want anybody to love you any less than so so much. Because I love you so so so very much."

Inside my eyes there were twinkling stars. She reached for them, for me, her wrists just barely above the surface. She couldn't swallow the entire ocean. She screamed, and she screamed, and she screamed. Then finally, she stopped.

TONESA JONES

Betty's Benediction

Betty came to the hilltop parish after Father Morris abandoned the downtown cathedral in favor of a small white church in Mandeville overlooking Lake Pontchartrain. She was too old to move and didn't trust the levies to hold back the next flood. God had spared her house during the hurricane, and she took it as providence that the Holy Spirit wanted her to stay put.

But her ungrateful children moved to Nashville and left her to deal with the house alone. Her good-for-nothing husband, may he rest in peace, left her more debt than insurance money, so she rode across the bridge every day to work at the Piggly Wiggly in Poulin.

Ray Rawlings was the store manager, and he worked her to the bone for a paycheck barely worth more than the paper it was printed on. But she didn't complain. She unloaded boxes, stocked the selves, cleaned shit and used needles from the bathroom stalls, and chased down would-be thieves, hefting all 115 lbs of her body at their ankles to tackle them to the ground.

Her efforts earned her a chipped tooth and no dental insurance to repair it.

Poulin shrank in the decade she worked at the Piggly Wiggly until too few people came through for Ray to afford to pay her.

She spent her last check on a week's worth of groceries and a pack of Newports and sat on her front porch, midday on a Wednesday, digging a spoon into a half gallon of ice cream with one hand and puffing on a cigarette with another. She had been a good wife to Carl, and the bastard didn't have the decency to be worth enough to pay for the porch she was sitting on. She snuffed the cigarette on the rotted planks and shoved a spoonful of butter pecan into her mouth, the cold shooting pain into her chipped front tooth.

She could have married John Boothes who moved to Houston and made it big in oil. His wife wore Chanel, and their kids went to an expensive out-of-state college in Wisconsin. Betty thrifted Walmart clothes from the Salvation Army and couldn't send her girls anywhere. Another promise Carl didn't keep to her.

She watched the ash from her cigarette blow in the wind and wondered if it would be worth it to set the damn thing on fire. A developer was shopping around, waiting for her to fall far enough behind to snap up the property for a bargain once it was foreclosed on. She'd rather work the rest of her life at the Piggly Wiggly than give that balding white man the satisfaction of taking her home from her. She was glad to be the fly in his pudding, spoiling his plan to buy the northern half of the island to develop into a luxury island resort.

Who the hell would come to Shortditch anyway, she thought bitterly, taking one more bite of ice cream before her stomach started protesting. But a resort would pay better than the Piggly Wiggly or any other shop in town. The only other place good for cash was Mama Rey's place, and Betty wasn't about to start shaking her ass to make her mortgage payment.

Something wasn't right about that house with all those women living together. *I ain't a pussy eating dike*, she thought, remembering what she overheard from a trucker one time at the Piggly Wiggly about Mama Rey's girls.

"They were touching each other damn near completely naked," the man had said to Ray. "Just baby oil and a G-string on."

Men flocked to the downtown cathedral for those damn shows more than they did for service when it was a proper place of worship. Men just like her husband Carl, the lying cheating sonofabitch. She still remembered the first time she caught him behind the smokehouse with a woman nearly half his age, his thighs tucked underneath her skirt.

She spat on the ground and crushed her forehead in her palms. She could have forgiven him the first time, even the second time, with the thick-bottomed red-bone girl who came to audition to be in Bo Weep's show, but the baby was the last straw. Fifty-two years old with an infant and the mother barely old enough to rent her own apartment. Her daughters didn't know about their half-brother. The kid was nice enough, ferrying passengers, packages, and dead folk back and forth from Shortditch to Poulin. He took care of Frank, her brother-in-law who was a decent enough man not to tell his nephew all about the messy affair.

Word came from the sky and interrupted the grumble of her thoughts. Mud-splattered pages descended to the trees like a flock of mourning doves. A handful of pages landed at Betty's feet. She picked up a sheet. It was a page from a hymn book and scrawled in dark red ink in big bold letters: God has answers on the Hilltop.

Betty looked to the sky. Clouds had moved in and turned the day into mud. The sugar in her stomach was slowly souring, and her belt dug into her belly uncomfortably. At the very least, maybe she could get something to eat up on the hill. When her mother took her to revivals in Jackson, it was an all-day affair in a hot one-room church with windows and doors open, sweat staining the collar of her shirt, and always a big spread of food afterward.

She deserved one night not worrying about fixing dinner. She deserved one night when someone finally took care of her.

The "hill" wasn't much of a hill at all since most of Shortditch was flat like the bottom of a bowl, but the tent sat at the edge of a cliff that overlooked Pearl River. Betty arrived in the only Sunday dress she owned which was half a size too small and squeezed at her bloated midsection.

There were a few dozen people there, and an organist playing up a storm in the sweltering heat of the tent. She stood in the back row, her large tote tucked full of zip-lock bags under her right arm so she could carry a plate or two home for the evening. The folks were in a frenzy, clapping their hands in time to the music. Some stomped the ground, sliding out of ties and top buttons, undoing cufflinks, and rolling down pantyhose. Betty began to clap her hands, smiling at the hymn she recognized. She hadn't been to a church since Pastor Morris had left. She hadn't had time to. But now she had all the time to bring her burdens to the altar.

A man emerged at the front. He wore a black robe embroidered with black crosses and his eyes were shielded by black glasses even though the day was dim and sunless. Betty had never seen this man in Shortditch, but that didn't mean much. Betty didn't see much of anyone, having worked every day in Poulin until she got fired.

Even with his eyes shielded, this man was commanding. With a sweep of his arms, the tent fell silent, and the energy of the room began to shimmer.

"Praise the Lord, saints."

A chorus of praise-the-Lords echoed back. Betty quietly whispered it under her breath.

"I've been brought here with a message of prosperity. God does not forget about the places man has neglected. I heard that the good people of this town were left without a shepherd to lead the flock, so I came to answer the call. I see sin has moved right on into downtown Shortditch. Right on into God's house in the form of that ill-reputed club owned by an affront to our Father and that mother of Jezebels."

There was a chorus of Amens, and Betty nodded her head.

"I'm here to tell you the shepherd is back in watch, and not one more sheep shall fall into the grip of a wolf. Not one more fox gonna come clawing in the hen house. Every soul under my voice, you have sanctuary."

People screamed Amen and rose to their feet. Betty nodded fiercely. She needed sanctuary. Her home was not her own and nearly lost to her. Her husband had broken his vows and stole her peace night after night. She had not slept in their marriage bed since the night she had caught him behind the smokehouse. *Fuck him*, she thought. She was tired. The years of holding everything together sinking into her bones, sagging her in the plastic folding chair that could barely hold her weight.

The lie weighed on her lungs like death. She let Carl die in peace, still a good father to their daughters, still known as a good husband to her neighbors. She worked to keep the house that was meant to be a legacy for their girls. But he had left her nothing but more work to do.

"Who here is in need of healing?"

Hands raised in the air. People hummed the pain like a hymn. The pastor walked the aisles, brushing the tops of people's heads as he walked by. Some grabbed at his sleeves or grasped his hand when he touched them. Betty kept her hands tucked in her lap, massaging her belly which was churning and gurgling. She closed her eyes, willing her stomach to go silent. She knew better than eating all that dairy, but she needed something to ease the sting of being jobless right before her next mortgage payment was due.

She didn't realize the pastor had stopped in front of her until a church sister with an accordion Barack Obama fan tapped her on the shoulder.

"Sister, he is waiting for you."

She opened her eyes, and the pastor was kneeling in front of her, his hands outstretched. Her tired sweaty face was reflected in the glare of his sunglasses. She took his hands, and he stood up and led her to the front of the congregation.

"We have a new member in our flock today. Tell the good folks who you are."

She stared out at the crowd and suddenly felt embarrassed in her too small dress with her purse full of Ziplock bags.

"My name is Betty Knight."

Her voice sounded small in her ears, but the congregation clapped for her, their sweaty smiles warm and welcoming.

"Welcome, Sister Betty. Why have you come seeking sanctuary on the hilltop?"

She stared at the faces waiting for her answer. She was ashamed to admit she was hungry and tired and just wanted a warm meal she didn't have to make. Her back hurt from years of lifting boxes and scrubbing shit from toilets.

"I'm tired," she finally answered, "I'm tired and there is no family for me. I don't see my children. My husband is resting in God's embrace," *or the devil's*, she thought to herself, "and I just don't want to be alone. I want to keep my home. I want someone to love me."

A dam broke in Betty's heart, and she buried her face into her hands, tears raining from the gaps between her fingers.

The pastor wrapped her in his arms.

"You are not alone," he whispered into her hair. "I will never abandon you the way your family did. This is your family now."

Betty felt heat bloom in her belly like she hadn't since she had conceived her second child with Carl. At that moment, she remembered she was a woman, not a workhorse or maid, cleaning up after men too busy to love her. She let her body melt into the pastor's, sunk her tear-stained face into the nook of his shoulder, inhaling the spice of him. He smelled like fresh-cut pine and tobacco smoke.

He lifted her chin, and she stared into her reflection.

"We will take care of you."

And they did. They fed her fat buttered rolls, baked chicken, and mashed potatoes and paid her no mind when she loaded her bag with half a chicken and a basket of rolls.

The pastor spread the word about the impending foreclosure and suddenly the problem disappeared.

When he came to call at her door after a fortnight, she didn't hesitate to let him in her home.

"Call me Marcus," he had insisted. He slid off his sunglasses and stared into her eyes. She had never met a black man with electric blue eyes, cool and intense like the hottest part of the flame. She melted under his gaze and let him slide up the hem of her skirt as her pantyhose rolled below her knee. She had warned her daughters about being this type of woman, indecent with men calling on them at unrespectable hours, but this was a man of God. Maybe after all those years of suffering her husband's infidelity in private, God had decided she deserved a reward.

She let him divide her, her ankles tangled in pantyhose, legs raised to the sky in prayer, her dress hiked over her hips and pulled beneath her breasts. His cold belt bucket cut across her thighs, leaving scratches, but she clawed him in return, murmuring his name like a benediction until he collapsed on top of her. He kissed her throat and left her with the mess he made.

And this became their ritual.

Him coming in the middle of the night. Her cleaning the mess left on her sofa, and soothing ointment on her scratched thighs.

She wanted to tempt him with more of her skin, each night greeting him with less on. The pantyhose was gone. Then her button-up Sunday dress. Finally, she answered the door in just a slip.

Each time was still the same routine. Him pushing her to her back. Pulling the hem of her slip up and the straps down. Him unzipping and slowly pushing his weight into her. Kissing her throat when he was done and leaving.

This was enough for Betty.

The congregation paid off the remainder of her mortgage. She owned the house she slept in and earned a modest salary at the clerk's office in Poulin. And Marcus still came at night and laid her bare on the sofa. She collected the money for the church during Sunday services, crawling the aisles with a wicker basket sweeping up crumpled dollar bills and change. She sweet talked strangers traveling through Poulin to visit the Hill Top Church, bribing them with slices of pecan pie. The more strangers she brought with her to Sunday services, the longer Marcus would linger on her sofa. The night she knew he was finally hers, he arrived at her home, the same late hour past midnight, and pulled her into his lap, his lips on her collarbone.

"You are a blessing, Sister Betty." He did not slide the slip away but asked her, "Can I come to bed with you? I didn't want to disturb the place you made with your husband."

She stood up and pulled the Pastor into her bedroom, "This was not my husband's bed well before he left this earth. I have waiting for someone worthy to share my bed with."

She took him into her bed, cold sheets tossed to the side, and their bodies became wet with heat.

In the morning, he began telling her secrets about Shortditch that only a man seated over the whole island would know.

"Those same people that came around when the bank was ready to foreclose on your house are swooping around the church like vultures. But we own the land. Building or no building, they can't snatch up what we got. No they gonna pay us."

Betty turned to him, kissing his chest. "But where will the church go if you sell the land?"

Marcus smiled, "Back where it belongs in the heart of downtown. Our cathedral."

"The one owned by Bo Weep?"

"The very one. I'm not worried about Bo. Because what we are owed will be returned to us."

Years had passed, and Betty knew the developer had moved on, calling the island "swamp water." The land the church sat on was worthless. Betty had been collecting money for years and had counted nearly every dime in the building fund. Over half a million in tithes and donations, not counting the checks the Pastor collected in private meetings with out-of-towners. Betty didn't ask where the money was going, and the Pastor rewarded her loyalty.

This is when Betty began to discover the difference between the pastor, leader of the Hill Top Church, and Marcus, the man who slept in her bed every night. The pastor dressed like death and hid his eyes behind shades, pulling miracles from thin air. But Marcus was an old man scheming to get what he felt he deserved, and Betty was fine to go along with his schemes as long as her bills were paid and her pantry was full of food. She asked no questions, even as she saw how he looked at other women, his hand lingering on their shoulders as they knelt to pray. Marcus was not a loyal man, but he took care of Betty better than her husband did, so she said nothing.

He showed up one morning with a body in the bed of his old Chevrolet truck. The boy was probably her daughter's age. He was covered in mud and smelled like an open sewage drain. She pinched her nose at the stench.

"I need you to keep him here." Marcus pleaded. He dragged the young man up the steps and laid him on the living room rug, sketching a line of mud from the door to the sofa.

Betty sighed and went to the kitchen for a sponge and bucket. She was getting tired of cleaning up after men.

"For how long?" she asked, scrubbing.

Marcus was halfway out the door, calling over his shoulder, "I'll have him out of here in a day or two."

The boy was alive, she discovered as she bent over to drag him to the cellar. Instead of heaving him into the dark dank basement, she dragged him to her bathroom, stripped him out of his clothes, and laid him in the bathtub. She wanted a son, but four pregnancies and two miscarriages later, she had two daughters who looked just like their father. Of course, the moment her husband laid in another woman's bed, he produced a son, another thing he failed to do for her. But Marcus had brought her a son. She washed him and ran water through his dark hair that curled up in little ringlets.

This boy reminded her of the man she had fantasized about who came to fix the HVAC at the Piggly Wiggly. That man was the color of toasted straw and always smelled like motor oil and peppermint. He'd see her in the back, greet her with accented English, then get to work while she unloaded boxes. On his break, he helped her shelve canned goods and shared his lunch of pozole and cochas with her. He told her his wife had made it for him, and Betty longed to have someone at home making meals for her with the love and care she could taste in this man's lunch. When she got home in the evening and laid on her empty bed, she imagined him there to fill it, the sweet words flowing from his native tongue.

This would have been our child, she thought, looking at the boy in the tub, the porcelain turned black from the grim she rinsed from his body. When he was clean, she swaddled him in towels and rolled him onto a sheet to drag him to the back room that used to belong to her daughters.

She tucked him into the pale pink blanket, his wet head still wrapped in a towel. She would not let Marcus take the boy, she decided. His brow suddenly furrowed, and he began to toss in his sleep. Betty tightened the blanket and smoothed his forehead with her hand.

No, she would not let Marcus take him. This was her baby boy now, and she would do anything to protect him.

BANCHIWOSEN WOLDEYESUS

Jaana

Before I said the words no *Gurage* woman had ever said before, we were not allowed to sit on the three-legged chairs in our park. There was centuries-old tradition we were expected to uphold.

***

In midafternoon, before I said the words, in front of my father's hut, in my father's hug, a sob escaped my throat.

"What did you say?"

"Ab... Abel has another wife." The lump in my throat grew bigger, starting to hurt.

My father shook his head. "That can't be—"

"I just talked to him, he confirmed it." The lump in my throat sank to the pit of my stomach.

"What're you talking about? You are his wife."

"He also has another wife!"

My father shrank—what I was saying registering in his brain. He thought I married Abel because he was from the city; a man from the city would never marry another woman while he was married to me. He was right, but I married Abel because I loved him too—and that love was my choice.

"I'm going to divorce him."

Thinking about the words that came out of my mouth, words that would make me a divorced woman at twenty-three, I didn't notice my father's silence.

I looked at his face—his face, which had become white.

"Father?"

"You can't divorce him."

From afar, I watched myself wondering how my heart

kept beating, how my legs were still standing. Inside I was shattering—my father's words shattering me. After I returned from the city, I'd talked about women I'd met with my father, women who only have one husband, women who can go to a court and divorce their husbands if they want to.

"Father, what're you saying?"

"Our tradition..."

My father's shoulders hunched as if they were a painful weight. In his face was a thing that made me ache, made me want to shake him, it told me even *he* couldn't protect me from the elders.

I stared at the fig tree in front of my father's hut and saw Jaana, the terror on her face, it was like she was sitting beneath the tree right now, her dark eyes staring at me with so much despair.

When a strong wind shook the tree's leaves, I looked back at my father. He reached for me, but I ran to the tree and dropped on the ground. My thumb pressed the inside of my left hand and I cried—I cried so hard I feared my heart bursting out of my chest just from all my crying.

***

One morning, when Jaana and I were fifteen, her father raised his hand, standing from his chair. Most of the town's people had gathered in her father's hut for coffee. I sat on a three-legged wooden chair next to Jaana, who sat near a fireplace pouring boiled coffee from a *jebena* as high as possible into demitasse cups.

"I have chosen a husband for my daughter!"

With her father's announcement, Jaana's hand trembled. Years later, I would see Jaana pouring hot coffee into cups after her father announced her wedding. Years later, I would ask myself why I sat in that wooden chair in silence rather than do almost anything else. I would know what I avoided, what I feared. To anger *Gurage* elders felt like the most dangerous choice to make.

That morning, while everyone laughed and talked about the Habesha Kemis Jaana was going to wear on her wedding day, about her future husband's father who owned most of the town's land, no one noticed her tears falling.

Days after her father's announcement, Jaana became quieter, staring off into a distance. Nobody asked why.

Only later did we realize we should have asked.

***

When I arrived at Joka Court, the local court, I told the receptionist my name.

I had made an appointment to talk to a judge on the previous day. Even though I stayed in my father's hut—I didn't want to go to my hut and face Abel—I didn't talk to my father for weeks. I was torn by his stricken face. My father had held my hand and walked with me to school, even when *Gurage* elders told him girls do not go to school, they belong inside a hut, near a fireplace cooking *gomen* for their fathers, brothers, and husbands.

When the receptionist called my name, I stood at the door of the judge's office and a sadness came over me. I thought about my one-year-old marriage. And those moments when we sat by the fireplace in our hut, Abel's dark eyes catching the orange and red of the flames, giving his eyes a beautiful reflective flicker as the fire cracked into another piece of wood. It had been three weeks since I confronted Abel and his eyes had looked away. Now I wondered if I should wait for more days to decide.

Inside the judge's office, an old man—probably in his late 60s, a round-framed eyeglass on the tip of his nose—sat on a chair, writing on a large paper.

"Sit," he said, indicating the chair in front of his desk.

When the judge looked up, he stared—curiosity written all over his face. His curiosity made me think a woman never sat in the chair I was sitting in now.

"Why are you here Mrs.—?"

"Call me Taci,"

His eyes widened. Then he looked at me like he expected me to apologize. Why would he—oh, I had interrupted him. I thought of Jaana. The feeling of being a free woman had been strong in us, we had wanted to speak back to any man who told us our only job was to cook *gomen* and bear children, even when that man was a family member.

"Taci?"

I blinked and looked at the judge. He was looking at my hands. I shoved them between my legs and struggled to speak as if I was speaking for the first time.

"I want... I want to divorce my husband."

Leaning back on his chair, he laughed. The walls of his office echoed his laugh, elders who came before him laughed with him. "I'm glad I didn't retire this year, I would have missed this. I want to divorce my husband, she says. I can't wait to tell this to my wives."

Of course the judge had wives. What did I expect? For centuries, if Gurage men could provide for their wives they married as many wives as they wanted. I was surprised at myself when I didn't run away from the judge who was laughing at me.

I leaped from my chair. "I want to divorce my husband."

The judge stopped laughing. His look—which was pitying me now—made me want to crumble on the floor. I wanted to ask him about his only granddaughter. Before she was married a month ago, they walked, grandfather and granddaughter, side by side, around town. I wanted to ask the judge if he wondered why the whole town had not seen his granddaughter since she was married, if he wondered about her husband—if he would ever allow his granddaughter to walk beside him around town.

"Did you get permission?"

"The only permission I need is mine and I have it."

"Did you get permission?"

"From my husband?"

The judge nodded.

"I don't need his permission."

"Listen, Taci"—the judge leaned forward—"you can't divorce your husband, you know that. Get permission."

A week before Jaana's wedding, her brothers sat on three-legged wooden chairs, like they always did before they went farming, waiting for Jaana to bring them *gomen* with *kocho*. That morning, her brothers called her name.

There was no answer.

That day, when my father and I looked for Jaana all over town, we met two women who sold leaves of false banana trees who told us they'd seen a girl who looked like Jaana. She'd hopped in a bus in the town's bus station. When we asked the women where the bus was going, they said they didn't notice. That night, when Jaana's father asked my father for any news of his daughter, my father did something that would have made the elders throw their hands on their heads if they knew.

***

"I'm gathering women at Tiya Park on Saturday," I said.

My father's neighbor, in her 60s, listened. For the past three days, I had thought about what I was going to do next. If I divorced Abel without his permission, everyone in town would shun me. Worse, I would be branded with *Anqit*—a curse *Gurage* elders believed in. I didn't know what made me think I could change centuries-old tradition. I was invisible here, I had no voice. That was when the idea of gathering women had occurred to me.

After a few minutes, my father's neighbor told me to leave her hut. I couldn't blame her. Her husband, who had three wives, owned the highest number of cows and horses in town. My father's neighbor was his first wife.

Defeated, I sat on the grass in front of the woman's hut. When I'd talked to the woman, even though her eyes never left her front door, I could tell she wanted to know more. But when I said *women's rights*, she'd looked at me as if I spoke a different language.

"You can't sit here, my husband will be home any minute now." My father's neighbor had run toward me, her eyes looking frantically around her.

I scrambled from the grass, picking twigs from my skirt. "If you change your mind, there's going to be—"

"I heard you. Leave now."

The next woman I spoke to was milking cows. She didn't look at me, but another woman, knitting across the hut, looked at me with curiosity. From her grey skirt—the holes on it showed she wore the skirt for many years—I gathered she was a maid. "What are you doing?"

On my way to the next hut, I met Jaana's father and three elders who walked with him. One of the elders, who seemed to be in his eighties, wobbled toward me, clutching his crutch. He was the one who asked what I was doing. I was about to bow when I remembered these elders were there the morning Jaana's father announced her wedding. They'd put their hands on their laps, palms upward, without once looking at Jaana. I was raised to bow when I came across an elder, but now my shoulders refused to bend.

"I'm gathering women at Tiya Park."

The elders threw their hands on their heads. "You can't do that! No woman ever sat there before."

I stood still.

They were right. Only men sat on the three-legged chairs in Tiya Park, located in the middle of town. But something, something more troubling, was troubling me now. Even after what happened to Jaana, even after I went to the city, even after I listened to women in the city talk about these things they called women's rights, I never opened my mouth, to question this tradition that did not allow women to sit in our park. What did that say about me?

"We know you went to a big school far from here," the elder with the crutch said.

I said nothing.

"That doesn't mean you can gather women in our place!" Jaana's father spoke for the first time.

There was something about his deafening voice that made me want to run away from him.

One time, Jaana and I were in her father's hut reading a book my father bought for me. We didn't think he would come home, in the afternoon he was always farming. When his voice came through the door we shoved the book under a mat and bolted to the back of the hut—to pretend we were near the fireplace cooking all along. While we waited for her father to leave, Jaana's index finger tapped her lap *one two three*, *one two three*, one two three.

Now, I wanted to ask him if he ever thought about Jaana, if he regretted his decision to marry his fifteen-year-old daughter to a stranger, but I could tell—his eyes threw thousands of arrows at me—that nothing had changed since the morning everybody in town shouted Jaana's name, the mountains echoed her name, and we waited for her to walk through town bobbing up and down, like she always did. But no girl bobbed up and down that morning.

"Men gather at Tiya Park, why can't women gather there too?" I said.

***

On Saturday morning, I arrived at Tiya Park one hour before the time of the meeting. I walked to one of the three-legged wooden chairs, moved to sit, and stopped, bending without sitting. Even though there was no one in the park, I looked around imagining elders, their hands on their heads, and noticed a huge cow nibbling grass. He stopped nibbling and looked at me. His big eyes seemed to ask, *What are you doing here?* I forced myself to sit, pressing my thumb on my left hand and imagining Jaana—walking between the false banana tree plantation, approaching Tiya Park, sitting next to me, telling me she didn't hate me. If she were here she would close her eyes and tilt her neck backward to feel the sun on her face.

"You're actually doing this?"

I didn't hear Abel approach me. Since I found out Abel also had another wife I'd avoided him.

"Look around, no one is coming," Abel said.

I didn't look around. I knew there were no women in the park. I'd talked to forty women. When I went to their huts, I went in the afternoon—a time when their husbands were farming. Still, every woman I talked to had looked over her shoulder.

I craned my neck upward to look him in the eye. "I'm going to divorce you."

"You're not."

"Watch me."

Abel's eyes widened before something on the grass stole his attention.

I looked down.

A stick. *Was he—?*

Abel and I stared at each other.

I knelt, picked up the stick, and said, "Do it."

I thought Abel could not hurt me more than he already had, but when he looked at the stick in my hand, a struggle written on his face like he wanted to snatch and hit me with it, the face I loved looking at became this town's face—a face telling me I couldn't divorce my husband.

One hour later, my father, Jaana's father, the judge I spoke to in Joka Court, and the three elders I met—who told me I couldn't gather women at Tiya Park—walked toward me. Six more elders walked behind them.

"I called this meeting..."

No one was listening to me.

"I called this meeting for women!" I shouted.

The elders stopped talking and looked at me. "You're the only woman here," one said.

"Let us discuss..." another said.

I stared at the elders who took over my meeting—talking about their precious land and cattle.

The women from the city had made it sound so easy. When they told me that I need to speak, they'd sat with their husbands, or men they called friends, and they'd talked and the men had listened. I tried to imagine men in my town sitting next to a woman, and listening to her. I couldn't imagine it. The only man from this town who had ever listened to me was my father, and now he sat next to Jaana's. That night, my father hadn't told him what we'd heard from the women who sold false banana trees. Now, when my father caught me looking at him he stood.

Jaana's father grabbed his hand.

When loud voices came from the false banana tree plantation, I expected more elders coming to join the others.

As a man and a woman approached Tiya Park, I recognized the woman's voice.

"I'm going to the meeting," the woman, my father's neighbor who'd told me to leave her hut, said.

"You can't do that!" The man I recognized as her husband said.

"You!"

When the man advanced toward me, the woman stood in front of me. "I'm going to have a meeting with these women," she said.

"What women?" The man pointed at me. "There's no woman here except her."

The woman looked around. "The two of us will have a meeting."

Silence followed the woman's defiance. I couldn't look

away as she looked her husband in the eye. It wasn't until she clutched my arm and tears filled my eyes, that I allowed myself to imagine being able to divorce my husband without the elders cursing me. Maybe I wasn't the only woman who wanted to be my husband's only wife.

The woman and I were turning away from her husband when the maid, wringing her hands on her skirt—the same grey skirt she wore when I met her last time—walked toward us. When the elders' eyes landed on her, she stood still.

I held on to her hand and looked the elders in the eye. My father—still standing, Jaana's father still holding his—was trying to hide his smile. *And was that—?*

Something about the judge's face made me stare. He was looking far away, I didn't know where until I realized he was looking in the direction of the hut where his granddaughter now lived. When he turned, he looked at me with a look I'd never seen on an elder's face before. It was familiar, but I couldn't remember where I'd seen it. Then I remembered—the faces of men in the city had the same look when they talked to women.

The elder next to him nudged his arm, and the judge blinked.

The look was gone.

***

At first, we were only three. A week later, another woman would join us. The entire time, she sat on the grass looking over her shoulder. Days later, she would come to the meeting with three others.

At first, we would sit on the grass. Then I would sit on the three-legged chair and the women would shout my name, looking over their shoulders. When I continued sitting on the chair, they would stare at me and look over their shoulders, until one day, I would arrive at the park and find them sitting halfway on the three-legged chairs.

At first, we would sit in silence for hours. Then I would start talking, and the women would listen without speaking, until one day, a mother of three fifteen-year-old girls spoke.

Jaana's father would come to the park to tell us we were not allowed to be there. Sometimes while he told tell me that lightning would strike me, his eyes looked toward the mountain—and I could swear he was thinking about his daughter, until he'd turn his head, point his finger at me, and say *You will lose your mind one day.*

I would look at the women around me, realizing I would now risk everything for myself—bear the anger of Gurage elders, their curses, even if I had to look at the sky for the rest of my life—but I'd looked at Jaana sitting beneath the fig tree in silence.

One week before Jaana disappeared, she'd wanted to talk to me.

"Taci, I don't want to get married," she said. Her face, haunted with despair, looked like a ghost. She grabbed my left hand and squeezed it.

When I winced, she didn't hear me. Her index finger pressed into my soft skin one two three, one two three, one two three. With every press, I heard save me, save me, save me.

I'd sat beneath the fig tree waiting for a miracle to drop on my friend's lap, and the shame of this truth never left me.

CHINWE I. NDUBUKA

The Limits of Math and Life

"GPS Signal Lost."

Reggie raised his brows. That a female voice had emanated from the pocket-sized navigational unit adhered to his windshield to announce its uselessness was parabolic. It irritated him almost as much as the cartoon rendering of his car on an otherwise empty stretch of road. Vehicles hemmed him in on all sides. It seemed the June sunny sky had brought everyone out. An SUV cut in front of Reggie, narrowly missing his bumper, and swerved again to the lane on his right, almost colliding with an accelerating Mustang.

"People," Reggie muttered.

His seventy-two-year-old heart was under enough stress keeping up with Atlanta's I-75/85 Saturday morning traffic. For someone speeding along an unfamiliar six-lane highway, he needed enough notice to know when to change lanes and advance to an exit ramp. He did not need a breach in satellite technology.

He'd checked out of his hotel with enough time to drive to the airport, return the rental car with a full tank of gas, get through airport security, and walk with dignity—not huff-and-puff this time—through the world's busiest airport to his gate. Glancing at the illuminated digits on the car's dashboard, he estimated he had ten more minutes of this jaw-clenching commute. In a few hours, he would celebrate Father's Day Eve with his family.

Eating out the day before Father's Day was a tradition they started a few years ago after waiting almost an hour at a restaurant for a table large enough to seat their party of nine. This year, all thirteen of them were coming and Reggie had made dinner reservations. He couldn't afford to miss an exit. When Andy, his middle child, texted a week ago that he and his two children were coming, Reggie had typed and erased three versions of a response before the one his wife typed and sent for him. Reggie hadn't seen Andy or his kids since Andy's divorce three years ago. By Reggie's calculations, Shawn was nine, and Eden was now five.

"GPS Signal Lost," the voice repeated as Reggie entered a tunnel.

Red tail lights glowed brighter in the grey enclosure smeared black in areas and dotted by two rows of lights. Engines hummed deeper and unseen traffic rumbled above. A moment later, Reggie burst into the sunshine and the GPS worked on relocating itself. Reggie stretched his fingers one hand at a time and curled them again around the steering wheel.

A conference had brought him to Atlanta. Though a retired math professor, he kept his brain sharp by playing the trivia television show *Jeopardy!* from his living room and attending conferences of mathematicians. He loved math because it was reliable. Three times seven always yielded twenty-one no matter who solved it. He was most likely the oldest attendee at the conference, but it was crucial if he was to live—actually participate in life—to a hundred and one.

Since his introduction to prime numbers in elementary school, Reggie had thought them honorable to stand alone, divided only by themselves and the number one. In college, advisors helped him tailor his classes to support a career he could live with. It was then he began to romanticize the idea of crossing over his own centennial, but not too far over. 101 thus became his ideal resting age. But more recently, living long meant a chance to create enough good memories so no one remembered him with disdain when he was six feet under.

"Keep right," the GPS said. "Keep right."

The white dashed line between Reggie and the lane on his

right quickly morphed into a solid V, guiding the right lane away from him.

"Keep right," the GPS insisted.

Ring. Ring. Reggie's cell phone rang in the console in a tone he'd chosen from a time when telephones had stable square bases and handsets fit securely within one's grasp.

"Keep right."

Ring. Ring.

Reggie turned on his blinker and glanced at his rearview mirror. He started to move across the V, but a quick turn of his head revealed a white pickup truck in his blind spot. He swerved left. By the time the truck whizzed by, the V had fully developed across the asphalt.

"Keep right."

Amid the noise of his phone, the blinker, and the GPS, Reggie yanked the steering wheel right and crossed over to the other branch of the V. A horn blared. Reggie's phone dinged as a text message came in. Then another. Glancing down at his phone was all he could bear to do.

He imagined it was his wife, Gina, at a grocery store calling to ask if he wanted chicken breasts or drumsticks for the grill on Sunday. Or whether he thought their youngest, Hannah, would be okay if Gina bought snickerdoodle cookies for Toby, the one-year-old baby of the clan. Or some such thought. Last month, while grocery shopping, he'd feigned interest as Gina considered design, durability, and unit price of paper plates for her book club.

Reggie heeded a sign for a gas station and exited the interstate. His heart rate decelerated with the car as he pulled into what turned out to be four gasoline pumps and a dinky cube of a shop smattered in posters. He parked in front of a vacant pump and reached for his phone.

The small screen within his palm reported two missed calls, one voice message, and two text messages. Starting with the voice message, he listened to his doctor say he wanted to talk about Reggie's physical test results. Dr. Monroe's tone was conversational, pleasant even, but Reggie had his doubts. Dr. Monroe usually mailed Reggie's results and added a handwritten note confirming Reggie was fine. Two years ago, Dr. Monroe's right leaning cursive advised Reggie to watch his salt intake. Gina had seen to that. Maybe the follow-up call was a new effort to maintain relationships so the clinic didn't lose patients to self-diagnosis websites. The other missed call was from Gina who'd also sent a text asking when Reggie would be home. He frowned at her words. She had a copy of his itinerary. The second text was from Hannah yelling, *CALL MOM.*

Reggie didn't realize he held his breath as he dialed until his first word came out as a gasp.

"What's wrong?" he asked as soon as Gina picked up.

"Dr. Monroe called. He wants to see you."

"I know." Reggie waved at the gas station attendant watching him through the shop window. He hoped the attendant understood he planned to buy gas.

"Have you called him?" Gina asked.

"Not yet."

"I'm worried."

Dr. Monroe had been their family doctor since Hannah returned from college with chicken pox and their then doctor was on sabbatical in Asia. Reggie had seen Dr. Monroe calm in the face of Reggie's scared four-year-old granddaughter with appendicitis, accompanied by her crying mother and his panicked wife. Dr. Monroe had not blinked during a physical when Reggie confessed he was under stress, burning through money, spending it on legal issues, and smoking pot in motels while separated from his wife who worked for the county court clerk. That was twenty years ago. Dr. Monroe was never ruffled and not one to convey fear, but Reggie shared Gina's uneasiness. His annual physicals usually came and went without ceremony.

Dr. Monroe picked up on the third ring.

"Hello Doc. It's Reggie."

"Sorry to bother you on the weekend. I've been looking at your bloodwork and I'm a little concerned. About your cholesterol."

The jelly-filled Danish pastry, large coffee, and fruit cup Reggie enjoyed for breakfast at the hotel café came to mind.

"Your levels are quite high."

"Heart disease high?" Reggie ran his hand over his full head of mostly grey hair.

He looked good, not the stud he was fifty years ago, but good. Never mind that he wore glasses. He walked upright and carried a suit well. He played with the grandkids and enjoyed fresh air. But so did his uncle decades ago when he keeled over during Reggie's college football match and died soon after of a heart attack. Reggie remembered his aunt clamping her hands over her mouth, tears sailing down her face while his father and the school medics did what they could.

Dr. Monroe cleared his throat. "It looks that way, but I want to run a few more tests to be sure. Gina said you're out of town."

Reggie didn't want to become a statistic. He had things to do and places to be, lost time to make up. He was having so much fun being "Gwapah," Toby's version of Grandpa. Toby's latest thrill was sitting on Reggie's foot, clinging to his leg like a koala bear while Reggie walked about the house. His own mother was going strong at ninety-eight.

"Reggie?"

"I'll be there first thing Monday morning."

Reggie refueled the car and paid at the pump. He would wait until he got home to tell Gina. Or maybe after the kids returned to their homes. He didn't need everyone fussing over him.

Starting the engine, he watched the GPS unit come to life with a flash of color over its black screen. He turned off the engine. At this point, after all the phone calls, he was behind schedule. He needed a backup plan in case the GPS threw another fit.

Reggie headed inside and walked past shelves of snacks and car fluids to where the spying attendant, a bald bearded man, sat behind a half-wall topped to the ceiling with glass. "I was hoping you could tell me—"

The attendant passed a slip of paper the size of a fortune cookie message under the window.

The tiny text on the paper began, *Turn left onto road. Merge onto I-85S...*

Reggie chuckled and a smile softened the attendant's face.

"Thank you, sir." Reggie waved the slip and left.

"Turn left," the GPS commanded as soon as he pulled out of the gas station. It functioned all the way to the airport.

***

Soon after leaving the security checkpoint, Reggie spotted a flight arrival/departure board. His flight's status—Boarding. He walked faster but soon gave in to short sprints through the teeming airport, thankful all he had was a carryon with wheels. Though his chest burned, he kept his mind on dinner and his eyes on the gate numbers. When his gate came into sight, surrounded by a mass of passengers unraveling like yarn into a slow moving single file, he resisted the urge to collapse onto the floor. Instead he leaned against a pillar and breathed deeply.

***

Reggie sank into his window seat and released a loud breath that barely but surely fluttered the dark hair of the woman seated in front of him. Passengers continued to file in, searching out seat numbers and scanning the people already seated. Reggie closed his eyes and focused on his breathing.

He was close to falling asleep when the slam of the overhead bin startled him. A flight attendant walked through the now empty aisle toward the front of the plane, shutting the bins as he went. The seat next to Reggie remained vacant, a rare blessing for his aching driving leg. He stretched out his leg and snapped his seatbelt in place.

About to depart on time, he typed on his phone. With a tap of his forefinger, he sent the message to Gina.

Her response was immediate. *Good. Toby is here.*

Reggie smiled and put his phone away just as a man walked up and set a computer notebook in the chair next to him.

While the newcomer stowed his carryon, Reggie straightened his posture. His knees dug into the chair in front of him, soliciting a partial turn of head from the woman in it. Just two hours.

The newcomer, with well-coiffed hair and a crisp white shirt over jeans that also looked ironed, greeted Reggie as he took his seat. He mumbled something over the captain's welcome spiel about why he was late. All Reggie heard from the captain was that Milwaukee had clear skies.

As the plane ascended, Reggie looked out the window of the gravity-defying cocoon and watched the earth disappear beneath clouds. He loved to watch planes navigate the sky. He couldn't say the same for his seatmate who opened his computer notebook as soon as permitted. One day, Reggie hoped to instill his reverence for innovation in Toby.

He contemplated in silence until flight attendants came by asking, "Pretzels or peanuts?"

"Salty and crunchy, or salty and crunchy?" his seatmate joked when the attendants were out of earshot. He had politely refused both.

"At least peanuts are protein," Reggie said, throwing one into his mouth. He saw no need to change to his diet until he met with Dr. Monroe. But the next peanut went straight to the back of his throat.

Reggie held his breath and sat as far forward as his

seatbelt would allow. He forced a cough that sounded like a whisper. From the corner of his eye he saw his seatmate turn.

"You all right, buddy?" the younger man asked.

Reggie held his mouth open, his neck crooked. No way was a peanut going to be the death of him. Despite his smarting eyes, he leaned his head all the way forward, resting it against the chair in front of him, and taking a quick breath, coughed again. It was a harsh sound that could not be ignored. The little sucker fell out of his mouth, onto his lap, and rolled to the floor. Reggie inhaled deeply and sat up.

"It almost went the wrong way," he confessed. "I'm fine though."

He noticed an attendant standing by the cabin divider wall watching him. Another approached from behind and offered him a cup of water. He took a sip and returned the cup. It was just a peanut, not a—

A weird sensation, not really a pain, more like squeezing, spread across his chest. He had not expected side-effects for coughing up a peanut. Now that he thought about it, only a sore throat seemed reasonable. So why did he suddenly feel out of breath sitting down? Was it the altitude? He recalled his sister-in-law talking about feeling dizzy on long flights. Reggie focused on his body. His chest rose and fell evenly with his breathing, but the weird sensation spread like a spider web reaching up to his neck and across to his arm. He shut his eyes and pressed down on his chest.

"Sir?" He recognized the voice of the woman who had just offered him water. "Excuse me."

"I'm an EMT," Reggie heard his seatmate say. It was as if angel wings had sprouted from his immaculate shirt.

Reggie felt hands—he assumed his seatmate's—press against his belly and release his seatbelt buckle.

"Buddy, tell me what you're feeling," his seatmate said. A hand rested on Reggie's shoulder.

Reggie groaned inwardly. He would rather not say. He hadn't experienced a heart attack before but with Dr.

Monroe's voice fresh in his memory, plus his age, he was scared. Downright terrified.

"Pain all over my chest and arm," he managed. "And here?" He rubbed his neck, confused. Visions of Gina, Toby, and his morning walks with the dog passed through his mind.

"You're sweating and having difficulty breathing," his seatmate said. "All symptoms of a heart attack. Get me aspirin."

Reggie didn't travel with aspirin. He had mint chewing gum. Much good that did him thousands of feet in the air. His heart sank as he realized he might not make it to Father's Day Eve dinner. This is it.

"Hang in there, buddy," his seatmate said. "You're gonna be fine."

Reggie heard mumbling. He couldn't tell if his seatmate was praying or conveying a dire prognosis to a flight attendant. Neither thought encouraged him. His hand was taken from his chest and enclosed around a tablet. He chewed it as directed. Then there was an oxygen mask, an announcement, and an emergency landing in Cincinnati.

***

Reggie's heart leaped Sunday morning when the door to his hospital room inched open and Dr. Perez peeked her head around with a smile. It could only mean one thing—Gina was here. Yesterday, Gina had texted him, We're coming even though it was not Reggie who informed her of his emergency admission into a Cincinnati hospital. He didn't see her text until after his procedure as Saturday's setting sun reached through the windows of his hospital room and hung orange rectangles on the milk-colored walls.

He'd been brought into the hospital by strangers. He'd laid awake on a table while Dr. Perez and other strangers worked on him, and he'd come out of it alive—for this he was extremely grateful—to no one waiting for him. Knowing

Gina knew and was coming to be with him had helped him surrender that night to the drowsiness of a long day and fading anesthesia. Sleep had been so-so, but today was a new day.

"You have visitors," Dr. Perez announced.

Reggie pushed himself up to a sitting position as the door opened to reveal Gina and their two daughters, the most beautiful things he'd seen in days. "Hey."

"Happy Father's Day!" they cheered softly, taking only a step or two into the room.

They stood like statues in the expanse of the grey speckled floor before Reggie realized they were staring at his pale blue hospital gown, the white sheets, and bedside buttons.

"I'm fine," he said. "Right, doc?"

Dr. Perez nodded and walked to the foot of his bed. "He's doing great. We're pleased with his recovery so far."

Lydia, Reggie's oldest, scared of horses but mother of a pre-teen, and owner of a dance studio in Chicago, approached slowly, her cork wedge sandals not making a sound. Her hug was gentle. She held onto him longer than he remembered her ever hugging him, filling his nose with a baby powder-like scent. He squeezed her arm.

Hannah followed, smiling through watery eyes that made his well with tears. "Dad, I'm so glad you're okay," she said, hugging him tight.

He rubbed her back. "Me too."

"The procedure—angioplasty, we call it—went very well," Dr. Perez explained. "When Reggie was brought in, the EKG confirmed he'd experienced a heart attack in the air. We performed the procedure to open up the affected artery and..."

Reggie watched Gina nod through the explanation with one hand anchored to the strap of her purse hanging from her shoulder. Her gaze shifted back and forth between Dr. Perez's gestures and him. He could tell Gina's brain was working fast, probably considering how soon he would get back to full activity, or how she could have been planning his funeral.

He reached out a hand to assure her everything would be okay. “Gina.”

“Reginald,” she said. “You have caused me too many heartaches to pull this stunt.”

Reggie raised his brows. His daughters gaped. Dr. Perez excused herself.

Gina continued. “First, you weren’t sure you wanted to marry me and we postponed the wedding after sending invitations. We had the kids and suddenly, you were hardly home. I thought for sure there was someone else, but the drugs and plagiarism were a worse nightmare.”

Her eyes were dry, her voice strong. The only good thing Reggie could find in this airing of their dirty laundry was that their daughters already knew his sins. The postponed wedding was a running joke that came up every Thanksgiving. He had come clean about the drugs, the plagiarism, and his suspended tenure his first night back at the house after living away for almost two years. The kids were in college at the time, but Gina invited them home for dinner. It was meatloaf. That night had been a circus of emotions. Gina and the kids fed off of each other’s anger and relief as he told them how he’d felt pressure to produce books like his peers to make more money. He’d apologized for all the pain he’d caused them and for the selfish person he became. He didn’t understand why it was coming up now.

“Gina,” he coaxed, opening out his fingers that had naturally recoiled. He twiddled them playfully.

“Mom,” Lydia said. “No one gives themselves a heart attack.”

Gina shot Lydia her don’t-question-me look.

“Honey, this isn’t how I planned to spend to spend Father’s Day,” Reggie said, ignoring a pain in his back. He needed Gina to know she had his attention.

She inhaled sharply, the prelude to a response. The door

opened and Andy walked in with a lunch paper bag. Reggie's heart skipped. In his dreams, his only son was always the lanky college t-shirt and sweatpants version. That was when they last really talked and kidded around, before Andy's girlfriend, now ex-wife, came into the picture. Now Andy stood before him with more bulk under his dress shirt and khakis, sporting a distinguished goatee. Reggie had heard second hand of Andy's post-divorce struggles and recovery.

"Hello son," Reggie said.

"Hi Dad."

Reggie watched Andy's gaze run over him, from his head to his covered feet. This was not the reunion Reggie envisioned. Andy hesitated, then walked up and hugged Reggie with one arm. His hug was feather-light.

"How are you feeling?" Andy asked.

There was a lot Reggie could have said. *Sore. Happy. Like I escaped death but maybe that was a mistake.* "Better. Sorry I missed dinner."

Andy shrugged. "We all did."

"Not just yesterday. The years before." Reggie turned to Gina. Her face was hard despite her skin's soft creases and the wavy hair that graced her shoulders.

He'd tried to make up for his blunders. As a retiree, he spent more time at home than ever before. He occasionally worked as a substitute teacher for supplemental money. He did house projects and babysat the grandkids. He took Gina on trips, most recently to Canada for their anniversary. What started out as self-inflicted penance had evolved into the joys of his life. It seemed he'd been alone in this thinking.

"I'm going to find the doctor," Gina said and walked out.

Lydia hurried after her, shutting the door behind them. Reggie sighed and sank back into the pillows.

"What happened?" Andy asked, moving Reggie's phone and glasses on the bedside table to make room for the lunch bag.

Hannah sat on the edge of the bed and took Reggie's

outstretched hand in hers. "Mom's just scared, you know. She was quiet on the drive down."

"She's boiling mad is what she is," Reggie said. He knew now she had not forgiven him in all the years he thought their marriage was recovering with the help of counseling, weddings, and grandchildren. "Give me some good news," he said. "How are the kids?"

Hannah and Andy exchanged glances as if they were kids and he'd asked who drew on the wall in crayon.

"Oblige me."

Andy settled into a chair. "Eden starts kindergarten this year." He held up a hand, spreading out his fingers. "She's five. Oh yeah. And Shawn is in love with a girl named Hayley."

"Is she pretty?" Reggie asked. "Just teasing, son. It's so good to see you."

Hannah tapped her phone fervently. "Elliot starts kindergarten too. We got him a Spider-Man backpack."

Reggie watched the door. He imagined Lydia walking in first with Gina reluctantly following behind.

"Dad." Hannah showed him a picture on her phone.

Reggie looked, reached for his glasses, and looked again at a photograph of Elliot modeling his backpack. "Nice."

Hannah's phone dinged. She tapped the screen and handed him the phone with a smile.

It was another photograph, this one of his six grandkids with Hannah's and Lydia's husbands, posed together on the couch in Hannah's living room.

"Just now?" Reggie asked. He turned the phone to show Andy.

Hannah nodded.

From the way they bared their teeth, Reggie imagined the kids had been instructed to say, "Cheese." Isaac, Lydia's twelve-year-old, full of long limbs, was the only one not smiling. He sat squashed against the left arm of the couch, holding a cell phone. Elliot, Hannah's middle child, leaned over Isaac's lap, interested in the phone. Reggie reminded himself to take Isaac fishing. Pulling trout out of Lake Michigan was sure to put a spark in the boy's eyes. Isaac's father, Bill, perched on the arm of the couch, was a malpractice attorney who spent quality time with Lydia and Isaac at Navy Pier, further south on Chicago's Lake Michigan shore. But fishing was not Bill's strong suit.

In the photograph, Toby sat on the floor, his eyes focused on the camera while his pudgy fingers clutched a red cube. Reggie smiled at his little friend sitting still next to Andy's Eden. At the sight of Toby's sister, Bethany, sitting pretty against the right arm of the couch, Reggie remembered the bicycle covered in bows in his garage. He and Gina purchased it as soon as they received an invitation for Bethany's seventh birthday party next weekend. The screen went dark and Hannah swiped her finger across it, restoring the image. Hannah's husband, Kevin, sat on the right arm of the couch, laughing. In the middle of the couch, nine-year-old Shawn clasped his hands between his knees. His gelled hair spiked up like a pyramid. After watching him dutifully help Gina set the table one Christmas, Reggie had predicted Shawn was the grandchild most likely to go into the military. Gina had laughed and said he had a rock star in him. Gina had also predicted Andy's marriage would not survive a second child, no matter how adorable.

"Thank you, honey." Reggie returned the phone.

He was grateful for instant photographs, for dependable sons-in-law, for a daughter to intercede on his behalf while the other remained at his side, for a son back in his life, and for strangers who helped strangers. He could do without the heart attack, but everything together made one hundred and one still a worthwhile ambition. Getting there was another matter.

His father passed away at sixty-nine. Just last year, Reggie read a poem at a friend's funeral. He'd lost classmates and cousins, and comforted his brother's widow while his own heart bled. He knew so many dead people. Then again, he may have very well lost his wife while she still lived and breathed. *Where is Gina?* She would have loved the photograph now studied by Andy and Hannah, their heads almost touching. He needed his family like he needed conferences where people enthusiastically talked about math's significance, his significance. He didn't consider himself a praying man, but at this point he wasn't too proud to beg. *Lord, help.*

It was Father's Day. They should have all been home, him flipping meat on the grill, the adults reclining in lawn chairs while the grandkids played. He didn't have an alternate plan. What had the kid who called him Buddy said? "Hang in there. You're gonna be fine."

"Hannah," Reggie said.

Both kids looked up.

"Please text Kevin my hello to pass on to everyone."

As her fingers flew into action, Reggie asked with forced humor, "Son, tell me you brought barbeque."

Andy shook his head with a soft smile. "Sorry, Dad. Healthy stuff."

The paper bag rustled as Andy unfolded the top and reached into it. Reggie pushed himself up again and Hannah rolled a tray table over.

CLICK.

The door opened and a smile lifted the corners of Reggie's mouth. Thus he welcomed Gina for the second time that day.

"Hi." Gina walked in slowly, staring at the lunch bag before raising her gaze to meet Reggie's. "Dr. Perez will come and see you soon. She wants you to stay another day before the long drive back." She glanced at Lydia, leaning against the door. "We're to keep stress to a minimum."

Reggie knew she would. He had other concerns. "Are we good?"

"All couples have tough times."

"That's not what I asked."

Andy opened a container to reveal a chicken wrap sandwich and a small tray of vegetables, fruits, and nuts. "No stress, remember. You just had a heart attack."

"Ah," Reggie said. "I wondered why I was here."

Hannah glanced nervously at Lydia. Reggie regretted his sarcasm, but honestly, he just wanted to simmer. He'd earned it.

"We'll give you some space." Andy spread out his arms and ushered his sisters and mother toward the door. "Let's go to the cafeteria."

Hannah was the last one to turn away from Reggie, filling his vision with backs of heads and backs of shirts and backs of legs.

"Stop!" Reggie waited for them to complete their 180-degree swivel before continuing. "Gina, Lydia, Andy, Hannah, I'm very thankful you all came and I'm alive to see it." He realized another blessing he'd not counted earlier. "Gina, thank you for the text yesterday. You know I don't like surprises."

"You're welcome."

In her subdued smile, he saw she meant it.

CHALISE LATIMER

Mother's Love

1504 S. Kingsley St.

Something was different. She stared up at the house. Six months had gone by since she last walked through the vestibule at 1504 S. Kingsley St. Sadie looked down at her feet and noticed the pattern in the brick sidewalk. The rain gave the bricks a glass sheen. Surely, Heddi was home. Candlelight still danced in the stained-glass window of the attic.

Two generations of Jones girls were reared in the Kingsley Street house. Sadie hated that house. There was an Ever-present horrible beauty about the house. It was in the black French garden Metre wallpaper. A beautiful mahogany stain on the hardwood floors. It was hidden under and within ornate Persian rugs. It lingered alongside you down the long hallway. Watched you from the chifforobe, breakfront, and sideboard. It even sat on the tiny table where the photograph sat. Convinced it must have come with the house. Sadie was sure she was the only one who ever saw it.

***

Better Life

Abner Jones, Sadie's grandfather, was a barber and he purchased the house from one of his clients. A white man who fell on hard times. He sold Abner 1504 S. Kingsley St. for a little bit of nothing. Enough to make it to a better life in Chicago. 1504 S. Kingsley St. was not much of a house, but it was enough to secure his piece of Americah. Enough of a better life to pass on to his daughters. Now, his only grandchild,

Sadie, owned it. Abner's dying wish..."to keep this house in our family. It will come a time when it will be all that we have."

Sadie did not want it.

Heddi. Hester Jill Jones. Her aunt. The epitome of bitch, ruled with an iron fist. She worked hard to make her daddy proud turning that modest four bedroom, three story row house into the beautiful showplace that it was. You were greeted by clean marble steps and gleaming hardwood floors. Welcomed with Persian rugs, chandeliers and candelabras, ornate bric-a-brac, chifforobes, breakfronts, sideboards and a fireplace. For Sadie, it was just a damn house that she hated to be in. The events and circumstances that we experience in a home, the things that are poured into us, that we absorb in silence as we go about our lives in the place where we are brought become a part of us. Permanently. Whether we want it to or not. That is why she decided to sell the house. It was time to cut ties.

Sadie was four when her mother left her in Heddi's care. Heddi's baby sister ran off to be a jazz singer; "following some yella nigger." That's how Heddi spoke of her baby sister, if she spoke of her at all. The only picture of Sadie's mother sat on a table, in the hallway next to Sadie's bedroom. You could say that Sadie's mother running off was the reason why Heddi did not trust Sadie. It was imperative that an eye was kept on the girl.

The long narrow hallways of Baltimore rowhouses that kept rooms very far apart created a massiveness. Rooms were situated at almost opposite ends of the house. The only peace Sadie could get were the nighttime hours when she was in her room dreaming of a life away from 1504 S. Kingsley. A life with her mother.

The eighth step in the staircase at the front of the house creaked when you stepped on it. Coming upstairs after hours was a task since it was forbidden to use the butler stairs off of the kitchen.

Heddi counted. Steps, creaks, panties, days in between menstrual cycles, menstrual cycles. Pieces of food, minutes it took to get to and from school, the store and Sadie's best friend Fielda's house. Fielda was the best friend a Sadie with a Heddi could have. Fielda died suddenly in her sleep when they were nineteen.

That was the year Sadie left Heddi's house.

She returned six months ago when she received a letter from Heddi saying that she was to come home immediately. She was dying and with only weeks to live, there were things she needed to know. About her mother, who Sadie believed was alive and well in New Orleans. When everyone was migrating to cities up north, Nina followed that "yella nigger" down South. This made Sadie sad, happy and angry. Sad because the one thing she knew for sure about her mother was that she left her for a man. Heddi made sure she understood that. That sadness sat comfortably beside anger. Why the hell didn't her mother send for her, leaving her to the counting, the accusatory stares of burning judgment when she could have been living in New Orleans with her? Her beloved mother. Nina. "Nina Esther is alive and well. I don't want to see her!" Sadie slammed her suitcase shut.

Sadie stayed in the Kingsley Street house with Heddi for six months after the urgent "I'm dying. I have a letter from your no good momma." At first, Heddi was the same bitch of an aunt. No surprise there, Sadie knew that it was just some ploy to get her back home. The way she left when she finally moved out had been abrupt. It was a stormy night, the rain hitting the brick sidewalk like bullets. With Fielda's death, Sadie had all she could take. Enduring enough to make her strangle her aunt. Heddi had turned colder toward her. Restricting as many moves as possible. To school and home. That was it. There was absolutely no reason to go anywhere else. Not even to the park that could be seen from the kitchen window. A girl of nineteen in the 1930's could get into a lot of trouble. The world was her oyster. There was so much life to live. A girl of nineteen blossoms at this time. Especially Sadie. She was in so many ways like her mother. In so many ways she was like Heddi too. That shook Heddi to her core. So, restricted movements were imperative.

Sadie learned to circumvent restrictions. Counted footsteps were a breeze, all one had to do was spike the tea. Or move the hour hand forward on the clock. When Fielda would come over to study, hidden among their schoolbooks were blank pages for writing poetry and songs, classes were cut to sneak to Cuban coffeeshop where the college guys hung out. Listening to them talk of literature and African culture made her yearn for to get to Harlem. They spoke of these grand creative gatherings. Salons they called them. Mr. Hughes, Mr. McKay, Mrs. Larson, and Miss Hurston. There were conversations to be had, to listen in on. Heddi could try all she wanted to keep Sadie bridled.

Randall was tall. Brown like a paper bag. With coal black eyes. Hair cropped close to his head with a butter knife part. He wore a tan suit with an olive-green shirt and a hat to match. His fingers were long, slim like No. 2 pencils. He had hands made for holdin' and a gapped tooth South Carolina smile. Sadie supposed that he had made it up here when everyone else was looking for a new freedom, although, he didn't have much of an accent. It is entirely possible that they were from the same place. Everyone was not an outsider.

Randall was something special. And it was like Heddi could smell him on Sadie, which was illogical because the only interactions Sadie and Randall had were short distances. When her and Fielda walked into a coffee shop, Randall and his group from the University were debating the importance of the Renaissance. Its potentiality of impact being that the major players only amounted to a handful of unknown starving artists. Could a small group of people have a big influence on the world? There was the "HELL YES! OF COURSE!" side, then the "We'll have to wait and see, could be" side and the skeptical, "How can a group of blacks influence a white country. That's unfathomable" side. Conversations among the members of the talented tenth were intriguing to Sadie.

The bell on the coffee shop door jingled, announcing the girls' arrival. Only Randall looked up. Sadie caught his eye. He smiled and then went back to the debate.

"Of course we can make a damn difference. Why are we even here if that's not the goal?"

"I enjoy what I do, man. I want to share it with the world," a fellow student remarked.

One of the girls in the group sucked her teeth. "Blue, please."

Sadie and Fielda stood there absorbing it all, until another group of girls who were also cutting class showed up.

Randall took no notice.

"Excuse us." A tall brown girl snarled as she pushed by Sadie and Fielda, making eyes at the fellas engaged in the debate.

It was absolutely impossible for Heddi to know anything about Randall. Randall knew nothing about Sadie. So how could she know? Either way, Heddi became more of a snow queen. Sadie needed to get out.

***

Balm in Gilead

The sound of Heddi's good china teacup hitting the floor woke Sadie up. Sound sleep was foreign at Heddi's. Lulled to sleep by Heddi's strained breaths, Sadie waited for pauses. Abrupt spaces between life and death. This is when Sadie felt closest to Heddi, when she was quietly breathing. Less mean-spirited bitch with good intention, more loving mother protecting her daughter. A pansy covered teacup crashing to the floor announced that death had arrived.

Randall was finally able to cross the threshold. Walk those marble steps into the subway tiled vestibule and into the sitting room now that Heddi was dead. Officially the house belonged to Sadie. She did not want it.

"It's beautiful, a great starting point for our life together. Your auntie left you a gift Sai. So what she was a bitch, we have a house now," Randall said.

If they weren't secret newlyweds, ignoring the remark would not have been an option. She was a new woman of the 30's. Her generation was making their own way. They were educated. The Renaissance, an explosion of colored creativity was happening. These young women were no longer dependent upon or obligated to do as they were bid by their parents and husbands. True, things were still difficult, which is why Sadie allowed people to make assumptions about her color. It made life somewhat easier at times. Various publications bought her stories. Earning her own money afforded her the opportunity to be freer. Life with Heddi would become a story now that she was dead. Gone to glory.

The arrangements were set in motion. Heddi had planned everything out. She was meticulous that way. Deep down, however, she knew that left up to that ungrateful chile' an in ornate pine box would be her final resting place. There would be no elaborate homegoing service. Just a simple goodbye. How could anyone blame her? Heddi did not. She knew her niece. She also knew that she would have done the same thing. Heddi was no fool. She knew exactly what she wanted. To ensure that everything was done right, all of the arrangements were taken care of. Every detail.

"Amazing Grace" to be played during the viewing. Blessed Assurance at the top of the wake. "Marching to Zion" on the procession out of the church. Black and gold casket. White lilies, gardenias. Baby's breath, daisies, roses. Proverbs 27:6

Absolutely no remarks, the eulogy is to be kept short and to the point. Death is a part of life. Obituary even shorter. Born Hester Jill Jones Sept 12, 1871. Died February 23, 1936, in Baltimore, Maryland. She leaves to mourn her, one daughter Sadie Rowe Jones. No mention of education, lost loves, or other family members. No social groups or affiliations, not even a church home.

What was placed in *The Crisis*, however, was totally different. A three-page spread on the philanthropic work of Hester "Heddi" Jones. A complete history of Heddi, a glowing report of her enduring deeds in the upliftment of the Negro. The colored people. They celebrated her work with wanton women, how she taught them the skills, brought those "loose women" to change their ways, turning them into "proper ladies." How, as a fixture in the local National Association for the Advancement of Colored People office, she supported the Civil Rights movement in Baltimore. Yes sir, Heddi Jones was something to make our race proud.

Memorial remarks were left by The Mitchells, The Jacksons, Mr. Thurgood Marshall, Mr. Charles Hamilton Houston. The Chissells. Her work on various Civil Rights causes and the betterment of Colored folks in Baltimore was accounted for and rightfully praised.

All of this was news to Sadie.

The article said nothing of how cold and detached she was toward her daughter, Sadie Rowe Jones. How she counted. The constant counting. Everything was counted. Steps. Minutes. Panties. *The Crisis* made no mention of how the only time Heddi spoke of her baby sister was to refer to "her following some yalla nigger"

The Crisis celebrated someone Sadie did not know.

"Atlantis," Sadie whispered. Still a secret, it was the last thing she said to Heddi three hours before she left this earthly place. Sadie climbed into the big queen-sized bed next to her dying auntie and whispered in her ear. "Atlantis." Her tone suggested *This. This you won't take away from me, you shall not force me to give this up.* "Atlantis," Sadie whispered one last time.

Heddi clenched her fist, closed her eyes and turned her head, feigning sleep. "Ungrateful."

Sadie heard her even though Heddi didn't utter a word. Sadie got up and walked out of the room.

Heddi's letter to Sadie was peppered with urgency. Sadie responded with that same sense of urgency. What was it that she did not know? How was Heddi planning to turn her world upside down this time? Her mother. Not dead. Alive. Living in NOLA. A Jazz singer. Living what has to be a glamorous life. A life away from Hester. Why now?

At first, Heddi was vague about Nina. A new piece of information each day, answering only two in-depth questions at a time. "T'ain't got time to talk about this Sadie Rowe. Get on out of this here room."

When Heddi was flustered, she lost all of her affluent Sugar Hill vernacular, reverting back to the dialect used in the dirt floor homes down in Fairfield.

Sadie could hear Heddi singing. At first she thought it was the electro phonograph playing, Heddi was too sick to get out of the bed to play it. Surely, she would have called on Sadie to turn it on for her. Sadie crept down the hallway to investigate. Once she got to the door, she recognized a sound she hadn't heard since she was a little girl. Heddi singing. Beautiful sounds of praise coming out of her mouth.

"There is a balm in Gilead"

Tears rolled down her cheeks as she listened to her mother Heddi make peace with lord. Singing Him a song of praise in hopes that she would get into heaven and walk around those streets of gold. In that moment, Sadie was filled with hate, she wanted to storm into the room and smother Heddi with a pillow. Heddi must have known she was standing outside of the room crying. So she sang louder. Sadie wiped her face and went downstairs to make Heddi's final cup of tea.

"There is a balm in Gilead," she hummed as she walked down the long hallway.

"Look in that bottom drawer of the bureau Sadie." Heddi said. "There it all is."

Sadie went over to the bureau with befuddled excitement. She ran her hand across the front of the carved drawers. Feeling the flower petals and stems. The raised ridges of leaf lines. The empty spaces that created depth and held layers of dust. She opened the drawer. It was stuffed with all sorts of paper. Mail. Postcards, newspaper clippings, certificates of birth and death. The headline read: **Nina Esther Jones. Jazz Singer Murdered by Boyfriend**.

"Hurry up now gal. Bring me them papers. All of them."

Sadie gathered up what she could, toting them in her arms over to the bed. It took two trips. For as precise and calculated as Heddi was, the bottom drawer was a catastrophe. A mess of truth in black and white stuffed into the bottom drawer of a bureau with carvings of delicate flowers. Excitement immediately turned into sadness. Then anger. If she read it correctly, Nina, her mother, died almost fourteen years ago. Right after she left Baltimore to be a Jazz singer in New Orleans. Why was she just finding this out?

Heddi started shuffling papers around, obviously looking for something. "Here it is, she said," handing Sadie a yellowed folded piece of paper letter. It was from Nina.

To my sweet, sweet Sadie,

Love is a mighty powerful thing. This is something that you will understand when you get older. It will drive you to do the things you think are impossible. Let it guide you. My love for you is so strong. That is why I have to do this. For me, for us, for love.

I will be back to get you once I am settled. Please remember that I did this because I love you.

Love always,
Mommie Nina

Sadie had no clue what to do next. Heddi grabbed the letter.

"She loved that no good son a bitch. That's the mighty powerful thing she was talking about, that's the mighty powerful thing that was her death."

Sadie sat, stunned.

"Give me that black book gal."

Sadie moved a bit, but not toward the book.

"Sadie Rowe. Hand me that there black book chile.'"

Sadie moved and found the book. A worn black leather-bound copy of the Bible.

"Why didn't you just say hand me the Bible, Aunty?"

"*Because.* It's just a black book."

Heddi opened the black book to the middle where all of the pictures were. Sadie picked them up as they fell out. She only recognized her grandfather. Heddi flipped back to the front where the records were kept. Names and dates. People she had known briefly, people she had only heard of in passing and people she would never meet. Among the names. Sadie Rowe Jones Born November 17, 1918.

"Bring me a pen."

Sadie found a pen, handed it to Heddi.

Heddi's slender dark fingers looked fragile as she started to scribble something.

In a slow, deliberate script she wrote: Atlantis Heddi Carmichael.

"Hester is an awful name."

NATHANIA SEALES OH

Porcelain Dolls

Tasoa Katigiri met me in my hotel lobby in Tokyo at 8am sharp. His navy blue suit was a decade or more out of style. Tucked beneath the lapels, a once crisp white shirt had faded to a yellow whisper and a wide brown and white striped tie was meticulously woven around his neck. Tasoa's face was tanned, round and partially obscured by a pair of thick black glasses. They too were round. When I first saw him, he sat in a curved lobby chair facing the bank of elevators with an erect back and a Nikon camera on his lap. He held the camera with fidgety hands and looked expectantly at each person as they walked past.

"Tasoa?" I asked.

He nodded and looked up with soulful eyes that reminded me of my grandmother, who was the reason we were connecting. The two met by chance on a Greyhound bus in 1958 on a trek from East to West, across the United States. My grandmother, up from Jamaica, was taking a break from her disappointing marriage and traveling to my eldest aunt's graduation from nursing school. Tasoa was on his first trip outside of Japan and was about to enter college in the U.S.

I like to picture the two of them huddled in a couple of seats toward the rear of the bus--both soft spoken and polite. Tasoa had a camera then too. He took pictures of my grandmother and the various depots and stops they made along the way. From what I can tell, across those freeway miles and days, they fell in love a little bit. I could see it in my grandmother's eyes whenever she spoke of Tasoa. She blushed and smiled coyly. She spoke of him often, and their correspondence through the years remained strong. Through the dusty sun streaked plains, as the narrow bus wound along the curves of three inky nights they talked and laughed.

"Thelma. That's a nice name. Where are you going, Thelma?" Tasoa might have said.

"California, for my daughter's graduation from nursing school."

"College? You have a daughter in college? It's not possible."

My grandmother would have blushed.

I picture Tasoa shaking his head and my grandmother leaning into him.

Over the course of those few days, they forged an unlikely friendship and a deep bond. They exchanged stories about their homelands and families, dreams for the future and a promise to stay connected. A promise they kept by writing lengthy letters and cards to one another for over forty years.

I asked my grandmother to tell me about Tasoa many times, and she begrudgingly obliged. The story that stood out to me most was her description of the moment they parted ways. The end of his bus trip came a day or two prior to hers. They exchanged contact information and a lingering hug. As the bus pulled away, Tasoa stood waving to my grandmother with tears streaming down his face. My grandmother also teared up when recounting that day.

"That's how I remember him. He had a beautiful smile. That silly camera hung around his neck bounced up and down as he waved. I remember thinking it might break off and crash to the ground. I felt then like I might have been crashing too. I watched through the back window of the bus to the spot where he stood for a long time, until he was just a dot on the horizon. I have never seen him again, but we've always written. *He* has always written."

Then she grew quiet, a soft smile tugging at the corners of her mouth. It was bittersweet, full of nostalgia and regret. I often wonder what would have happened if she had decided to get off in Amarillo or Tucson or Phoenix or wherever it was his trip ended. What if she had run away? Run from Aunt Dimps' graduation, her four children still in Jamaica, her husband that she may have fallen out of love with. I bet she thought about it. Maybe it was just for a second, but I bet she thought about it.

When I saw him sitting nervous and dated, I channeled my grandmother.

He had a nice voice. He spoke gently and carefully. "You are Thelma's daughter?"

"Granddaughter. My mother is her daughter."

"Oh, oh yes, yes. Grand. Granddaughter. I'm sorry my English is not so good. Your grandmother..."

His brows crinkled with worry that he wasn't getting it right.

"Yes, grandmother," I said softly, trying to match his tone, assure him.

"She is a lovely lady. Kind. Beautiful. Inside and out. You do not look like her."

Tasoa's r's and l's were transposed. I focused on the sound his misplaced letters made and tried not to be hurt by the fact he didn't see my grandmother's beauty in my face.

"I feel as if I know you," he told me. "Your grandmother holds big place in my heart even when many years passed."

"I feel like I know you too. My grandmother has told me many stories of your kindness. It's amazing to know you kept in touch for all these years."

Tasoa reached for a handkerchief he had tucked inside his suit jacket. He dabbed his eyes and nose.

"I have not had experience like this one. Have not many kind ladies like Thelma. She one of a kind."

"She is.", I said.

Tasoa spoke softly again, "You have time to come to my house?"

"Yes, I've arranged it with my work colleagues. I have the entire day."

For the first time a broad toothy grin spread across his face.

"This makes me happy."

"It makes me happy too."

Tasoa stood and smoothed his suit jacket. He switched the strap of his camera so that it ran across his body, bowed and swept his arm toward the lobby doors. He led me outside where the air was warm, slightly humid, and the city was alive. We made our way to a subway station a few blocks away and were the only ones speaking English as far as I could tell.

It struck me then as it did several times while in Tokyo that I was in a linguistic cocoon. The Japanese language became white noise. In the thick of people rushing past me on the streets, on the subway, on crowded elevators where I towered over everyone, it felt like a blanket of hush. Because I didn't understand a word, couldn't make out one syllable, the noise of conversation cancelled out. This was true of printed language as well. I couldn't read signs, inscriptions, or slogans sprawled across the city. As a result, my mind turned inward. I was a cocoon within myself. It wasn't until that morning when my eyes met Tasoa's that something broke open. A light began to filter through. The love and connection my grandmother felt for this man, halfway around the world, passed through me, and in some filial way I loved him too. I allowed myself to feel connected to someone who meant so much to someone else.

"I have party at my house this afternoon. It will be nice for you."

"Oh, that sounds nice."

"Yes, I have friends come. We have party. Listen music. Little food. Nice party."

"I look forward to seeing your home and meeting your friends. Sounds nice."

As we made our way in the subway, I couldn't help but notice I was the only Black person. Black pepper in a bowl of rice, but no one seemed to care. No one stared at me or really paid me any attention. I was just another brown girl tagging along with your average Japanese grandfather.

"You here for work?" he asked.

"I am, yes. I work for Cartoon Network and we are filming with a pop group. Hi Hi Puffy AmiYumi. Have you heard of them?"

"No. I don't think so. You like job?"

"Yes, very much. A lot of stress, but I like it."

"You must be very successful, yes? I bet Thelma is very proud of you."

At our stop, we walked up a series of stairs to a subterranean walkway that led to the front of a store that resembled a Mega Japanese Walmart. A group of people formed a haphazard line just outside the locked doors. A few minutes after we arrived, the doors opened and the crowd poured in.

We entered the super store and a sea of uniformed employees bowed rhythmically at the end of every aisle. The rhythm of the folding bodies was background to their hushed cheerful greeting.

"Ohayō gozaimasu," they crooned over and over again.

Mostly women, they held their hands together as they bowed. Their muted peach aprons stood in contrast to the vibrant packaging stacked in precise rows surrounding them. Their voices were restrained and quiet, in direct opposition to the sights and sounds near the Harajuku hotel where I was staying. Tasoa had led me from that crush of neon, arcade music and people to this Walmart dressed in pink.

As we walked past the rows of cheerful employees, I marveled at the size of the store. I couldn't see the end of it. It seemed to just go on and on. Tasoa weaved through the aisles with familiarity. We walked past the household section and made our way to produce. There were rows upon rows of brightly colored fruit stacked neatly. Some were scaled and prickly, others smooth and shiny. I smelled ginger and the sweet flesh of dragon fruit. Another employee stood with a tray of freshly shucked lychee. She dipped wooden tongs into a bowl of water, cleansing the utensil before picking up. She bowed her head and handed me one in a tiny paper cup. It was ripe and juicy, thick and fleshy, sweeter than the ones I'd had back home. The vegetables came in every shape: curled and straight, porous and stocky, long and thin, wide but small. Tasoa picked up several pieces of fruit, some vegetables, canned meat and put it in a cloth tote bag to be purchased. The cashiers were noticeably less friendly. They click-clacked on their registers like chickens pecking up seeds.

From the store, we caught a bus to Tasoa's village. It was a twenty or thirty minute ride that dropped us by a large lake. The path we walked was unpaved. The soft yellow dirt was moist from a light rain the night before. We passed several people as they walked along the winding path. Eventually we came upon a row of short grey buildings. At the second building Tasoa led me to a wooden gate which opened to a narrow gravel alleyway.

"This is home," he said as he ambled down the path.

Overhead sat a thick blanket of green and yellow from overgrown foliage. I could hear the stones crunching beneath my shoes, and it reminded me of the neighborhood roads and driveways of Grand Cayman where I spent my childhood. He stretched his arms out wide and spun around slowly.

"Welcome."

He led me up a small metal staircase and we entered his small kitchen. Just off the room was a set of Shoji screen doors Tasoa slipped through after asking me to sit at his kitchen table. A few minutes later, he returned. He had changed out of his suit and was wearing a simple olive hued kimono.

Tasoa had changed more than his suit. He changed the language he spoke as well. From that point forward, he only spoke Japanese. I'm not sure why. Perhaps he was tired of trying to speak English. Perhaps in his home he expected me to adapt.

Although I didn't speak his language, there was an understanding I can't explain.

He laid out the groceries along with several bowls full of fermented vegetables. He gave instructions on how to arrange the food on platters in hand motions and his native tongue. After a while a silence developed between us that was easy and comforting. It felt like we had known each other for years and needed no words. Perhaps it was the connection Tasoa had with my grandmother. They too forged a bond in a finite amount of time. Two, maybe three days passed as they got to know each other and developed an attachment.

There in his home, Tasoa gently leaned over and put his hand on my shoulder. He demonstrated how to toss the vegetables and open the canned meat. He smiled and patted me on the head. When I followed his demonstration, doing exactly as I had been shown, he laughed quietly and clapped his hands together. He seemed proud of the job I was doing. In a matter of hours, I became his dutiful daughter, he, the gentle father I had always wanted.

As we methodically scooped the canned meat, forming it into tiny balls and placing them in the middle of crisp lettuce cups, then spooning fermented vegetables on plates, I found myself reflecting on my real father. I wondered why we never reached this kind of unspoken ease. Early thirties, halfway around the world and still I yearned for my dad. A melancholy developed in the quiet, just as I wished it was my grandmother sitting at that table. Forty years or more had gone by since she had been in the same space as Tasoa. I felt guilty and honored to represent her and hoped I was doing her proud.

Later, Tasoa and I walked back down to the gravel alley beside his home. Several fan palms hung low over the path that led to a large backyard. There was tall unruly grass, patches of yellow dirt and several large rocks around the perimeter. Up against his back wall were several pieces of plywood, cinder blocks, and a bevy of tools that included a machete. We walked back to the alley, where he put the machete to good use and chopped down the palms. The air had grown more humid and I could feel a dampness on my forehead and the nape of my neck. With my own camera, I snapped pictures of him working, at times motioning for him to pose. He stood with his arms akimbo like a Samurai, the machete clasped, hanging low and back in his right hand. He had removed his glasses when we'd gotten home. He looked older, softer, kinder. After a while he collected pieces of wood from his backyard. He sawed them into varying sizes. Once we had a healthy pile, he positioned them on top of stacks of cinder blocks, forming make-shift tables. There were swaths of plastic, red if I recall correctly, that were used as tablecloths. It was a haphazard party set up that seemed somewhat dangerous, but beautiful too.

All morning and into the early afternoon, Tasoa worked. He was not a young man by any stretch, and yet he never stopped moving. Sweat formed on the edge of his greying temples and all the while he smiled.

As the sun began to sink lower in the sky, people started arriving. It was a menagerie of friendly faces. None that looked like mine, but still I felt welcome. A bookish sandy blonde man brought his violin and began to play for everyone, and all seemed right in the world. An impromptu concert in a garden of plywood, cinder blocks and plants. It was perfect.

Shortly after people arrived, I helped Tasoa carry the platters of food we'd prepared, down to the collage of tables.

Some of the party goers had brought sake and wine. I floated from table to table, pouring drinks and letting the wash of Japanese envelop me. Eventually, I sat at the edge of the party and watched Tasoa with his guests. He was loved and revered, it was clear. I wondered how he'd come to collect such an eclectic group of friends. It was a mélange of characters: young and old, quiet and lively, formal and casual. I longed for my own sense of belonging.

As the sun began to set, I knew it was time to meet my coworkers back at the hotel. Tasoa stepped away from his party to walk me to the bus station. Along the walk he still only spoke in Japanese. I spoke in English.

"Thank you for a wonderful day," I said.

He smiled and, as we reached the bus depot, he held out a small cloth woven bag.

"For me?"

He nodded, and hand motioned for me to open it up.

Inside were two porcelain dolls, dressed in intricate kimonos. One was slightly bigger than the other.

He tapped its head.

"This you give Thelma."

Then he tapped the head of the smaller doll.

"This you take Atlanta."

My eyes welled with tears. The dolls looked like antiques, like precious figurines that had been handed down from generation to generation. Their bodies were nothing more than hollow wooden cones wedged neatly into shiny black rectangular blocks.

"These are beautiful. I will take very good care of these and make sure Thelma gets hers. She'll love it."

We hugged, and I saw his eyes moisten also.

Just then, the bus pulled up. Several people boarded before me. I was having trouble leaving. I felt like I was straddling decades, continents, regret and hope. It was overwhelming to think how transformative this trip, this day, this time had been. I reluctantly climbed the steps and walked toward the rear of the bus.

I could see Tasoa waiting on the curb. As the bus began to pull away, he jumped up and down and waved feverishly. I watched him and that broad smile grow smaller and smaller. I couldn't help but think that this was the very image my grandmother had seen somewhere in-between Texas or Arizona just forty years before.

MEET THE CONTRIBUTORS

Bios

Candace Bacchus Hollingsworth is a fun-loving writer and policy nerd who thrives on coffee, whiskey, and connecting folks (but not always in that order). After nearly a decade in public office as a do-gooder and changemaker, she's returned to her first love—writing—to make sense of this crazy, beautiful world. Memphis-made and raised, Southern flavor is in her genetic code, and she writes essays at the intersection of Black womanhood, racial politics, and the pursuit of radical joy.

Shinelle L. Espaillat is a writer whose stories have been nominated for the Pushcart and Best of the Net prizes. Her work is forthcoming in Pleiades Magazine and has appeared in Torch Literary Arts, Tahoma Literary Review, Two Hawks Quarterly, Minerva Rising, Ghost Parachute, The Westchester Review, Cleaver Magazine and Midway Journal, as well as in the collections Ghost Parachute: 105 Flash Fiction Stories, Shale: Extreme Fiction for Extreme Conditions, and How Higher Education Feels: Commentaries on Poems That Illuminate Emotions in Learning and Teaching. She teaches writing in Westchester County, N.Y.

Tonesa Jones is an Atlanta-based editor and VONA alumna. She received her MFA in writing from Savannah College of Art and Design in 2017. Her writing is influenced by Black folklore, ghost stories, Jazz and the Blues, and the American South.

Chalise Latimer has been writing short stories. One day, one of the stories will become a novel.

Chinwe I. Ndubuka's flash fiction and short stories have been published in Interpretations, the anthology of the Columbia Art League, Well Versed, the anthology of the Columbia Chapter of the Missouri Writers' Guild (CCMWG), Evening Street Review, and midnight & indigo. "Week Two and Counting" won a themed flash fiction contest organized by the Daniel Boone Regional Library. Chinwe is a member of the CCMWG.

Damilola Omotoyinbo is a Nigerian Creative Writer and Software Engineer. She is a fellow of the Ebedi International Writers' Residency, the winner of the SprinNG Writing contest, a co-Winner of the Writing Ukraine Prize, a shortlistee of the 2023 Writivism Prizes, a joint winner for the SEVHAGE-KSR Hyginus Ekwuazi Poetry Prize, and a finalist for the 2022 African Writer's Awards. She has work published or forthcoming on Lolwe, Olongo, The Deadlands, Ake Review, AHC, Torch Literary Arts, Agbowó, NND Poetry Column, The Nigerian Tribune NewsPaper and elsewhere. Damilola studied Biochemistry and her happy places are Pinterest, YouTube, and The Church. She tweets @_Damilola_O.

Shari Lynn Poindexter is a writer in Los Angeles at work on a short story collection and a novel, both centering on the complexities of love and Blackness. She is a mother of five and is also a health care professional passionate about maternal and child care and pelvic health. Shari has a daily walking meditation practice that allows her to ruminate about crafting worlds and helps her ease her mind. Shari is a fellow of VONA, Wildseeds Writers Retreat, La Maison James Baldwin France Residency, Jeff Sagansky Harvardwood TV Writers Program, PEN Emerging Voices Fellowship, Napa Valley Writers Conference, and Squaw Valley Community of Writers Workshop.

Nathania Seales Oh, originally from the Cayman Islands, is a screenwriting professor currently living and teaching in Orange County, California. She earned her BA in Telecommunications from Pepperdine University and her MFA in nonfiction from UC Riverside's low-residency program. Nathania believes humor and authenticity are the key to great storytelling, which she brings to her poetry, screenwriting, and creative nonfiction, where her true passion lies. In between working on her first full-length memoir and bingeing comedy podcasts, Nathania explores the world through food and travel with her husband and daughter by her side.

Sabine Wilson-Patrick, originally from Barbados, is currently a literature undergrad at Cardiff University in Wales. She is a Best of the Net nominee and a Hay Festival alum. She is also the managing editor of Rover Magazine, an arts and culture magazine for LGBTQ POCs. Her work can most recently be found in Nawr Magazine, Ethereal Magazine and Aster Lit. Her performances can be found archived on her website: sabinewp.carrd.co.

Banchiwosen Woldeyesus (she/her) is a Black woman, a teacher, short fiction, and nonfiction writer. She has sworn to read books slowly, so she pretends she has all the time in the world, so she can read this story, at this moment, so she can savor each story she's reading, so she can pay attention to small things she might have missed if she read the story fast—like the way a writer describes the feather of a dead warbler in a short phrase. Her work appears on The/Temz/Review and is forthcoming on SmokeLong Quarterly. Her debut short story collection—The Town Under the Mountains: Stories—is currently out on submission. She publishes essays, flash stories, and curated reads on This

Precious Dark Skin, her newsletter on Substack. She's a Submissions Reader for Narratively. When she's not writing or reading or teaching, she travels to Tiya, the silent town her characters in her debut book call home, just to stare at the mountains. She lives in Addis Ababa where she teaches.

About The Editor

Ianna A. Small is the founder of midnight & indigo Publishing and creator of *midnight & indigo*, a literary platform dedicated to short stories and narrative essays by Black women writers. m&i is her love letter to Black women like herself, who long to reach the pinnacle of their purpose. As the executive editor of midnight & indigo, she oversees editorial and creative direction for the digital and print platforms in addition to their Writing program for Black writers. A media marketing executive, Ms. Small also has 20+ years of experience developing partnerships, distribution, and content marketing initiatives for entertainment brands including BET, Disney Channel, ESPN, ABC, FX, VH1, MTV, HOT97, and more.

An avid fan of Black and South Asian literature, Korean horror, and all things Jesus + Michelle Obama + The Golden Girls + cultural food documentaries, she dreams of one day running m&i from a lounge chair overlooking the archipelagos of her happy place, Santorini.

Ms. Small is a proud graduate of Syracuse University and active member of ACES: The Society for Editing and the EFA (Editorial Freelancers Organization). She is a granddaughter to Irma, daughter to Nadia, and mother of Jalen Anthony, who is simply: her reason.

Made in USA - Kendallville, IN
37974_9798991920810
01.02.2025 2107